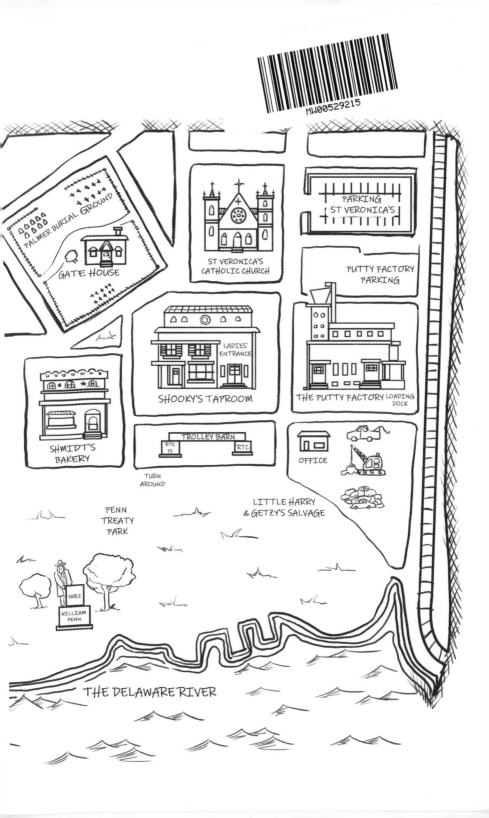

Big in Heaven ©2020 Stephen Siniari

Published by:
Ancient Faith Publishing
A Division of Ancient Faith Ministries
P.O. Box 748
Chesterton, IN 46304

ISBN: 978-1-944967-57-4

Library of Congress Control Number: 2020940565

Printed in the United States of America

*To my wife Margot
and my son Alexander*

With a prayer of thanksgiving for Katherine Hyde, editor of the blessed eyes, and the team at Ancient Faith Publishing. The after-liturgy coffee-hour tables and chairs at Saint Alexander the Whirling Dervish Orthodox Church would never have heard story one.

Rabbi, Raskova, Getzy and Little Harry, Elisa, and Teddy the Horse, all the approximately fictional characters who inhabit the fictionally approximate society of Naum's neighborhood, Putty Factory to Salvage Yard, Schmidt's Bakery to the Black Bridge, from Shooky's Taproom to Donahue's Funeral Parlor, down through the wrought-iron gates of Palmer Burial Ground, Father Naum and his beloved companions would have remained forever consigned to oblivion in the perpetual shadows under the Tunnel were it not for our Katherine, now granted honorary citizenship with all prerogatives, privileges, and neighborhood rights. —S.S.

Foreword

———•———

I have known Father Stephen for 26 years. He is my spiritual
father, a mentor and a friend. I worked at Covenant House New
Jersey with him as a pastoral minister and street outreach worker
and a fundraiser. I was ordained in his home parish, and we have
been through a lot together. I have served with him in the altar
and been with him in street fights between homeless youth.

For me, the value of Father Stephen's stories is that they are
a genuine expression of Father Stephen himself. Anyone who
knows him has experienced his gift of explaining difficult theological concepts through simple but poignant real-life examples.
The stories as theology speak for themselves. The characters are
colorful because Father Stephen sees, experiences and describes
life richly, while most of us experience life more blandly. It's like
seeing life in high-definition after watching it in black and white.

His stories begin to paint a new kind of icon, that of a truly
American Orthodox Christian, of regular people simply trying to
be or tragically rejecting being regular human beings, the kind
of people perhaps never even imagined by most American readers: Albanian Orthodox Christians from North Philly? A tough

ex-Soviet war hero, now an American humbly ridiculed in her own church for cleaning up dirty diapers? A friend of a suicidal black man searching for redemption in an Eastern Christian Church?

Fr. Stephen's stories offer something for everyone: they show the reality of church life to faithful people, and they present an image of holiness not imagined by people who are ostensibly without faith. The stories break the mold of what a religious or non-religious story ought to be. They are not moralistic (to drive away non-religious readers who simply want a good, true story), nor are they irreverent in their honest portrayal of the realities of life in the Church (to drive away a Christian reader). Rather they are just good, honest stories, and in being this they are sacramental, conveying and holding together elements of life that are seemingly disparate: imperfect priests, sad ruffians, petty church members, tough Russian émigrées, tragic black men . . . all become part of a series of funny, shocking, tragic and heart-warming stories—which convey deep realities of life.

Father Stephen's stories offer a unique Orthodox Christian vision of American life and a uniquely American view of Orthodox Christianity. Both are deeply needed in our culture today. They describe redemptive experiences mysteriously happening in the middle of a twentieth-century American city for all who wish to read with an open mind and heart.

V. Rev. David R. Fox, Ph.D.
Rector, Holy Trinity Orthodox Church, Randolph, NJ
Executive Director, Arm In Arm, Mercer County, NJ
Assistant Dean, St. Tikhon's Orthodox Theological Seminary

Contents

Big in Heaven

———·•·———

E VERY WEEK SHE WAS EARLY. Those who live farthest usually are. Who knows why? A bus. Then a long ride on the El,
probably forty-five minutes minimum on the elevated train, from
one end of the line to the other. One end of the city to the other.
And then another bus. A local, making every corner. Well over
ninety minutes one way for Raskova.

Probably she knit the hat, or bought it in the old country. That
style and that Cold War military color, the earflaps, it was obvious it wasn't intended for the fashion or the weather in our part
of America.

The long double-breasted coat, high boots, the tactical Middle Eastern head-covering, and mittens that could very well have
been confiscated from a Magyar conscript in the Siberian Garri-
son. It was clothing an inmate in a camp might have scavenged
from a pile of dead men's throwaways. Solzhenitsyn himself
could not have drawn a more convincing daughter of October.

No one knew she'd been a skydiver. No one knew she raised
pigeons on the small balcony of her inner-city subsidized high-
rise apartment. No one in the parish knew she was the mother of

a doctor, a son who never called her. No one knew every inch of space in her one-bedroom flat was covered with paper icons. No one knew she was lonely.

———·———

TALKING TO A FOREIGNER with a thick accent is an ordeal for some. Even in the church. Once after Liturgy she had me captive over a cup of green tea that tasted like topsoil. She brought it to church in an old glass jar with a faded pasta sauce label. She made the cross and swore it would cure my cold. In another jar she had an eggplant concoction so strong with garlic, even she leaned back and made a *phew* with both hands when the lid came off.

That was the time she told me she'd been a welder. If I understood her correctly, she had also been a tank mechanic in the army on the Eastern front and could fix any truck. Maybe the tea had a calming effect, but for whatever reason, I sat and listened. We ended up connecting. We became friends.

"I was best welder in Siberia," she told me. "Five years in a row. Give Raskova medal with kisses. They put banner, big, like covers-building big. With Raskova's picture, hanging down from ceiling."

"On the inside of the building?" I asked.

"Oh, no. Outside," she said.

"Hanging down from the roof."

"Yes. Roof." She smiled. She wasn't as young as she looked.

"Wow," I said.

"Yes, wow. Then I say to commissar, please, I'm sorry, comrade friend, I love big picture of Raskova. But maybe this time instead of best welding banner, maybe, if possible, little bit more money."

"What did he do?"

"She. She just look at me. Say nothing. Next day Raskova banner takes down. No more kisses and medals for Raskova."

The bread she brought from home—she told me she baked it—was perfect for dipping in the eggplant garlic puree. Before I knew it, we'd eaten all of it, the church hall reeked of garlic, and for a reason I couldn't figure, I was tipping my cup and wishing for one more sip of tea.

You didn't have to ask Raskova to help. Cleaning. Polishing. Carrying in or out. Any work in the church, the woman was a stalwart, a *tovarisch* you could count on.

No one knew her suffering. They never bothered to look into her eyes. It surprised me that most of the church folks at Saint Alexander the Whirling Dervish parish didn't even know her name. It wasn't anything they thought about. A whole group of people in our parish, Raskova included, from a whole bunch of different countries, just got tagged *the foreigners*.

I didn't know it was possible in our communion for an Orthodox believer to be regarded as a foreigner.

———•———

DANIELLE WAS A YOUNG WIDOW. Her daughter Alexa was still in diapers when Theo, her husband, was killed in the war over there. Sometimes the baby fussed a little during Liturgy, but that was normal. Kids in the Liturgy? Just how it was supposed to be. They didn't leave them on the shore in Egypt when Moses led the people across the Red Sea, and there were probably a lot of noisy little rascals in the ark with Noah and his wife too.

Upstairs in the hall, I was having a coffee and reading an

account of a Paschal celebration that made me proud and ashamed at the same time. I wondered if anybody else ever got so sad they couldn't breathe.

Danielle was across the hall at the after-Liturgy coffee hour, changing Alexa on a table. The poor kid, a widow at her age. She was still so shook, you could see her hands shaking. I thought of my mother wrestling with those cloth diapers, scrubbing them on a washboard, bent over the toilet. After Danielle left, I was thinking, good thing mothers no longer had to use diaper pins.

From where I was sitting, I couldn't tell one way or the other when the commotion started. My mind was already starting to wander down the shopping aisles. My wife Judy was planning another Sunday sojourn through the mall.

But there was stout little Mary—Nicky Zeo used to call her crazy Mary, but never to her face—an inch of roots white as scallion bulbs, and dyed black hair, always came to church in oversized gypsy skirts and embroidered blouses, wearing the same red dancer's vest, shouting like one of the produce hucksters who used to walk their horse and wagon through the old neighborhood streets. Even the deaf old men in our parish never yelled the way Mary was yelling, especially not in church.

"Get your foreigner ass over here and clean up this baby shit." Mary had one hand on her hip and a finger pointing right at our Raskova, standing at attention in her tight knit cap.

Raskova wasn't sure what was going on. I could tell by the strange smile on her face. I don't know if her English'd got to the point where she could recognize when she was being cursed. Could be she was happy and smiling just to have one of the American women speaking to her.

"I saw that other foreigner, the one with the twin babies, changing her kids right here on this table. This is foreign baby shit. She's gone. You're a foreigner. You clean it up."

I knew what Mary thought she saw. The girl with the twins, Eteri, she parked her kids on the table while she was dressing them to go. Both of the little cuties in those overstuffed snow-suits, two bundled red-cheeked dolls. But Eteri didn't change the kids' diapers there. That was our Danielle. Our American Danielle.

I watched Raskova take the rag from Mary. Her military coat with the scarf and mittens were draped over the chair at our table. I was reading the account she'd given me, by Gleb Alexandrovitch Rahr. Pascha at Dachau Concentration Camp. It spoke of the Orthodox prisoners celebrating the Paschal Liturgy in a prayer room borrowed from the Roman Catholic prisoners, using a single icon with a remarkable history and vestments made from sheets. The service was recited from memory in alternating Greek and Slavonic by Greek, Serbian, and Russian clergy. A service unique in the history of Orthodoxy.

She wasn't as young as she looked, our foreigner, our Raskova. When I stood to help her, mechanic's hands forced me down into my seat with an arm so strong it made me feel like a little boy.

"Don't worry, my friend, for Raskova," she whispered to me. "I clean baby shit. It small thing. You sit. Read." She said, "I am here," tapping the pages with socket-wrench fingers. "At Dachau too, my job, priest say, sew sheets for vestment, is very small, he tell me, but big in heaven."

Two Things

I KEEP THESE TWO THINGS *to remind me of my place in the neigh-borhood. Anybody ever gives me a compliment, I got the antidote. These two things, the license plate and the censer, keep 'em by my icon corner where I beg God for prayer. Constant proximity to these two things reminds me of the real me. It scares me, but I read and re-read the Book of Job.*

"COMPACT" WOULD BE A GOOD WAY to describe our Philadelphia Fishtown neighborhood, our church, and our lives together in what Father Naum calls *the covenant community.* Proximity in space, in time, and in relationship—being close.

Naum would say, "Proximity shows up pretenders."

He looks at 105-year-old Olga, one of the few *nunnas* remaining who was born in Albania, sees her in her favorite pearl dress, the one with the tiny red flowers, sitting in the front pew with her son, Teddy the Horse. Then Naum says, "That's why I'd never stand next to Mother Teresa, or Mother Stephania from the women's monastery, or our Olga, or any person who's really in tune with God. They'd show me up for the pretender I am."

It's hard to hide in a compact neighborhood. Walk the streets. You got Hollander's Drug Store on one corner. Catty-corner from that you got Spic N Span Cleaners, where single guys with a lot of expensive clothing keep their Friday-night outfits 'cause it's got bars over the windows, like a neighborhood Fort Knox for suits and shoes and shirts and hats and stuff ya wouldn't want disappearing from your basement room in Mom's house.

Down the street is Schmidt's Bakery, with George Washington cake—a spice cake, sort of, cut in squares. They got jelly doughnuts with any kind of jelly you can name. Pipe it right in for ya while you're standing there. Bread and rolls, cupcakes and butter cake, pound cake that people drive from all over the city for, making the whole neighborhood smell like your nunna's kitchen at Christmas.

Honest John's Grocery on one end of the avenue, Yankee's Grocery on the other, both grocers doing their best to keep it afloat against the big supermarkets moving in, people moving out and forgetting to pay their weekly tab.

Mom sends the kid down the block reciting the list over and over so he won't forget it: "Loaf o' bread, quart o' milk, stick o' butter, and a pack o' Chesterfields. Tell Honest John ta put it on the book. Daddy'll pay Friday from his pay envelope."

Honest John knows Daddy's good for it. Everybody knows everybody at the putty factory gets paid Fridays. And let me tell ya—ya don't pay John, word gets round the church.

No problem, though, for Ed Steinman, the butcher, where the blue-and-white checkerboard tablecloths out front match the curtains in his bay window, always shiny clean. You want fresh fish? You wanna sit and eat a sandwich two of ya couldn't finish on kaiser rolls Schmitty'd baked that morning? Custom cuts? Crown roast? Hammered-out flank steak for rouladen? Homemade wurst sausage? Not a problem. Mister S has ya covered. But no puttin' it on the bill there. Missus S just won't allow it, not even for Rabbi, not even for Ed.

Doctor Baks lives above his office. Jacob the shoemaker is tucked into three cozy rooms behind his shop.

Doctor Payne, the guy we call Painless Parker, the dentist, got an office in the other side of the duplex where he lives. "Hey, Lefty," he says, "ya want the kid to have novocaine? Cost ya an extra five."

Lefty says, "Nah, not this week, Doc. Envelope's a little short—no overtime this week." Takes a five out of his thin manila pay envelope and hands it to the dentist. "Told the kid to go easy on those Christmas candy canes."

Doctor Payne says, "Yeah, hell on the molars, candy canes. Novocaine ain't all that anyway. It'll toughen him up. Every molar drilled and filled, Lef," he says, "puts me one step closer to my houseboat down the shore." The cries of the wounded could be heard the whole length of the tunnel under the El down Kensington Avenue.

They say there's a bar and a church on every other corner in the old neighborhood. More like *every* corner.

We got the auto scrapyard too, where Little Harry and Getzy work, and a coupla funeral homes, like Donahue's and Wackerman's, but come ta think of it, I can't remember ever seeing a police station. A firehouse, yeah, but not the other.

Now if the churches have anything ta do with that, not having a police station, I couldn't say. Not that Officer Nardozzi don't walk a beat, but I'm pretty sure the bars don't have ta do with the police station being missing from the neighborhood either, if ya know what I mean? 'Cause I don't. Hey, I'm just a civilian works at the putty factory.

Shooky's Taproom, with the sawdust floor and the neon signs in the window, *Schmidt's Beer On Tap, Esslinger* with the pirate logo, and *Yuengling, America's Oldest Brewery.* Women never sit at the bar, not where we're from. There's a ladies' entrance on the side, tables with real cloth tablecloths where a guy and a girl can get a sandwich and a decent bowl of soup.

If old man Schmidt the baker could convince old man Shook the barkeep to say George Washington slept in one of the upstairs rooms up over the taproom, they could clean up selling those spice cake squares. They go good with cold beer. Not to people from the neighborhood, understand, but the downtowners who come looking for the Polish kielbasa the Cieweski family makes over on Orkney Street in their garage, or Ma Bunkowsky's garlic and butter crabs at Bunky's Crab Bar. Dirty or clean, make your fingertips sting all weekend, those crabs. Too bad Schmitty can't put all that on the bar top.

The Catholics got Saint Veronica's, with the rectory and the convent and the K-through-eight school—biggest cement school-yard in the city, even a tree or two in there.

Monsignor Maurice Truen has fifteen hundred families in the parish. He put a sign on the tree, it said *TREE* so the neighborhood kids'd know what it was.

At Emanu-El, the synagogue across the street from our church, Rabbi Aaron Strauss and his wife, Maureen, have a center with a basketball court and a gym. Teach Krav Maga, that Jewish martial art thing, got a Holocaust museum, a free medical clinic, and a day care.

Someone at the church, prob'ly the one ended up chasing Carol away with religious rules after she'd been gone so long, said there was actually a canon in the church rules that if a Jewish guy gets in the swimming pool, the Christian dude had to get out, and ya can't have a Jewish doctor either.

Rabbi has a swimming pool, a heated one, *and* a free clinic. Wha'd you fall out of a tree, or what?

We asked Naum about those canons, and Naum said, "Half the stuff I didn't know about the canons I learned a long time ago at seminary." So most of us go along with that.

The Holy Communion Protestant Church has a turret with a blinking blue neon sign on top, flashing out *Jesus Saves*.

The Miller Savings and Loan Police and Fireman's Benevolent Credit Union across the street has a counter-synchronized red flashing sign that says, *But We Give Interest*.

Pastor Calvin Hall went in to protest but relented when old man Miller threatened to cut off their free parking Sundays in the bank lot.

Our church is an old red-brick affair that had once been a Grange Hall and a music school.

Pauly, Jimmy the bachelor, and Nicky Zeo's pop, who they called Bucket-Head, and Coach Koulos dug out the dirt basement back in the day and carried it out by hand, a bucket at a time, so they could joist it up and reinforce the floors.

They put in the iconostasis. They rewired the place to bring it up to code so Lester's son Ralphie, the inspector, could give the nineteenth-century wiring a twentieth-century sticker.

Little Harry's father, Big Harry, climbed the wrought-iron fire escape, shimmied over the roof slant on his belly, and restrung the schoolhouse bell with cable wire so thick it only took one pigeon to panic when Little Harry pulled the bell, and the whole damn flock that nested up there took off for Atlantic City 'cause o' the screech the cable made when it scraped the metal flashing.

First time Naum saw them pigeons take off across the windows during Liturgy, he thought it was a miracle.

After Big Harry died, Naum climbed up there himself and replaced the cable with a thick rope he salvaged off a half-sunk hulk down on the Delaware. Big Harry's other son, Aleksander the stevedore, helped him drag the damn thing home and air it out. Took almost all of Lent.

Sometimes the ceilings leak and the floors creak, and the Teuta Ladies' Baking Society swear the day will come when they'll demand at least a new ladies' room and a commercial kitchen or go on strike and quit baking, but all in all, inside and out, you can tell Saint Alexander the Whirling Dervish is an Orthodox temple, in spite of the dervish thing.

Maybe it's the giant three-bar cross stuck up on the side of the building, or the icon mosaic of Saint Alexander an anonymous donor had installed up over the front door.

Naum and his family live next door above the garage that used to be the place Donahue's Funeral Home prepared people for their final tour of the neighborhood before heading over to the Orthodox section in Oakland Graveyard. Only time most of us ever got to ride in a Caddy.

There's just no hiding anything in the neighborhood. The city may be anonymous, but around the way, from the synagogue to the church, the doctor's to the drugstore, from the baker's to the butcher's, just ain't no place to keep a secret or hide.

At first Naum used to say, "Every Orthodox home, if it doesn't have an icon corner with a little censer, a Bible, and a bread seal for making the holy bread"—we call it the *meshe*—"well, then it's less than the domestic church it's called to be."

We understood about half of what Naum said when he first came to the parish. Later, after what happened to him, when we all thought he was gone, when *his* brain lost a little and *we* learned a little, we understood each other more on par.

And two things seemed to become important to Naum after that incident: a broken kid's license plate, kind of little plastic thing kids hang on the back of their bike; and an enameled hand censer, looks like a little cup on a stand, the kind with a cross on the lid that you stand on a table or up in your icon corner.

Naum had the busted-off lid, but the cross supposed to be on the top of the little censer ended up missing, and for some reason, after all that, he rarely talked about homes being *less than the domestic church they ought to be.*

Naum said, "I keep two things there where I pray, at my icon corner, and this quote from Saint Paul's letter to the Church at Ephesus: 'Fathers, do not provoke your children to anger, but bring them up in the discipline and instruction of the Lord.'"

He wanted his son Stevie to lose the training wheels on his bike. But the kid was afraid. Naum's wife Greta knew it. She told Naum to back off. Give the kid more time. He's only six. He'll do it when he's ready. Naum got mad. He yanked the kid off the bike, picked up the little two-wheeler, and threw it into one of those wire metal trash cans they have over there at Palmer Park, not far from the putty factory hospital, slammed the family in the car and drove home mad. Naum. Can you believe it?

———•———

HYPOCRITE. *I talked a good game about relating to everyone in love. Later, I went back and got the bike. What I did, the way I acted—I was wrong. The little plastic license plate with his name on it was broken into pieces. To this day, I keep it at the icon corner in our house. I apologized to him and to my wife. It still bothers me. Maybe he was six or seven.*

When he was sixteen I told him to start telling me no when he didn't want to do something, and that he didn't have to come to church anymore if he didn't want to. He hasn't been back since. My heart couldn't be any more broken, broken like his little nameplate license plate, what I did to my son. If I thought I was going to heaven, I'd trade places with him in a minute. The boy's my heart.

For if a man cannot manage his own household, how can he take care of God's church?

Saint Timothy read that, and he probably heeded Saint Paul.

My wife has her way of letting me know when she's not happy—if I've been spending too much time away from home or with a particular person. I realize now she has good instincts. But I was such an idiot, I used to actually pray and sort of give God an ultimatum: "If she doesn't back off, I'm gonna take it as a sign to give up on this whole thing."

Talk about tempting God. One time she got me so mad I walked away from the icon corner and slammed the door. The mini-censer— looks like a little lidded cup on a pedestal, with a cross on top, beautifully enameled thing from Greece—comes crashing to the floor. Ashes and sparks and incense all over. The lid snaps off. Could never find the cross. It busted off and went who knows where. I keep that broken censer too, up there on the icon corner. My wife never came to church again after that. Why come to church when you live with the head guy and know he's a phony?

If anyone does not provide for his own, and especially his own household, he has denied the faith and is worse than an unbeliever.

NAUM READ SAINT PAUL'S LETTERS to Saint Timothy again and again, maybe understanding a little better what the Fathers meant when they said, *Read for salvation, not for knowledge.*

Doctor Baks knows all the details, says it was pretty bad, that undetected blockage. The rest of us just know Naum died for a while. More than twenty minutes is what we were told, no heartbeat, no breathing.

Good thing his wife was there to call them.

Ray, Jeff, and Tyler, the EMTs from our neighborhood firehouse, and the two cops from the 26th District, Sullivan and Dempsey, they came—quick, too. Did CPR, the defibrillator paddles, the whole bit.

Nothing.

Got Naum to the ER. Same deal.

Told *Priftereshe*, the priest's wife, he was gone.

Then something happened Naum won't talk about, or else we'd be doing the memorial prayers for Naum.

She's the one, Prifteresha Greta, his wife, when he was lying there in the CICU under all the tubes and electronic monitors, who went home to their icon corner and found the license plate and the note that explained why he would never get new vestments or a cassock and wouldn't get a new tabletop censer, the fractured pieces of the little boy's license plate, hidden under the doily crocheted by our Antigone when she was 103.

———

I KEEP THESE TWO THINGS *to remind me. Anybody ever gives me a compliment, I got the antidote. My reality diptych.*

One thing I've learned after years of funerals, if anyone starts out a eulogy with, "And he was a great provider," that's not a good sign.

I may have been able, by God's mercy, to provide an adequate life for us in terms of material things. I like the word modest, *not up there with the richest in the parish, a few steps maybe above the poorest.*

But these two things, the license plate and the censer, constant proximity to these two things, remind me of the real me.

I am a failure as a husband, as a father, and as a priest, my inadequacy clear when it comes to being a provider of spiritual truth, a healthy icon of what it means to be a disciple of Jesus Christ, of His patience, longsuffering, forbearance, and love.

My wife is the censer. She takes the heat from the people when I mess up, and from me especially, from my charcoal-black heart. She turns the rocks I throw into incense, and prayer continues to rise from her. I found a note she wrote after she stopped attending Liturgy. It said, "I still love the Theotokos."

She makes our meager income work, protects the kids from my ignorance, anger, and arrogance, makes a home, makes it all rise up before

God like a prayer, and I broke it, snapped the lid off, lost the cross, fractured the precious vessel that birthed the prayer of our life together.

My son no longer needs the training wheels. He told me, "Pop, the words of faith aren't something I study. I eat them like the bread and wine. They're alive inside me."

My awareness of my failing makes me know I'm not worthy of my calling. There is only one priest, Jesus Christ. Any man who would seriously think of himself as priest, guy's got to be—well, who am I to judge?

Looking at these two things, and meditating on what I did behind them, exposes the truth of my selfishness when it comes to my relationships, my obedience and responsibility as a husband, as a father, as priest of my own household, and as priest to God's people in our compact little neighborhood and our church community.

So, I look at these things, and when I look around at Liturgy on Sunday, at all the families together, and it's just me, nobody from my house in communion with God, or at least with me, I know I have no one but myself to blame.

People get wounded along the path on the journey of faith, and at my house, I did the wounding. And any wounds I have are mostly self-inflicted—I have no doubt that I'm a failure in all four categories.

Husband.

Father.

Provider of a living example of spiritual Truth.

Priest.

So, knowing I'm a failure, and maybe because of it, I keep on keeping on. Nothing to brag about except having nothing to brag about, knowing I'm nobody's judge, worse than an unbeliever.

All this makes me reflect on how many times I've easily given up on people and organizations, on the Church, maybe on God even, how many times I've been dissuaded by hypocrisy in others. I have to stop and tell myself, "Who in the neighborhood hasn't been a hypocrite or a pretender from time to time? What person being honest with himself isn't dealing with inner contradictions in one area or another? Maybe we all got to take a turn wrestling with those angels."

So then I gotta think, how do I, a natural-born hypocrite, respond when I'm abandoned for hypocrisy by other hypocrites? Do I double down on hypocrisy if I don't stick it out with them?

I tell myself, "What else ya gonna do, Bud, give up on love, end up alone, and give in to . . . what? Or give in to Who?"

When my actions contradicted what I said I believed to be true, I was cut off as a hypocrite by those I loved.

Because of me they abandoned their hope in Him who is love and truth—I understand that too.

And through this suffering I've developed a reluctance to sever a relationship because of apparent inner contradictions in the struggle to love. Life's a mixed bag—the wheat and the tares grow up together.

I admit, there are betrayals that produce irreparable cosmic ruptures. But as long as the relationship remains good at the root, it's gotta be worth the struggle.

I pray to see the other, and be seen by the other, beyond facts that may seem to betray love or contradict truth.

When it comes to hypocrisy or contradiction, what level of severity merits everlasting fissures in the fabric of our shared being?

I feel alone at Liturgy without my family and ask myself, ask God, Must I be forever ordained to eternal separation?

Every day I pray that if somehow, in ways that are known to Him alone, He keeps me in Christ, it may be that my wife and son—if I *can hang on to them, if they'll continue to hang in with me, even by the last thread of love we share—it may be that even in our common woundedness, He will keep us together in the never-ending day of His Kingdom.*

———•———

NAUM OFTEN TALKED OF JOB.

For His eyes are on the ways of man, and He sees his every step. There is no darkness nor deep shadow where the worker of iniquity may hide himself.

No, Naum. No hiding anything in the neighborhood. The city may be anonymous, but around the way, from the synagogue to the church, the doctor's to the drugstore, from the baker's to the butcher's, just ain't no place to keep a secret or hide.

"Proximity shows up pretenders." Always said it, old Naum, now didn't he?

An Ordinary Sunday

N OW YOU KNOW THE ONE DEACON, not Dionysios, our protodeacon. He has two boys, Ezra and Isaiah, who serve in the altar. Their mother is the dark-haired petite girl, Diakonia Elizaveta—not that family.

I'm talking about the other deacon, Donat, married to Diakonia Anthia. Girl so sweet-natured and smiling blonde, even on ordinary winter Sundays when everybody's got their shovels and rock salt ready and the sky looks like it's about to burst a gut with snow, in comes our Anthia to light her candles and kiss the icons in the narthex, and the sun himself can't resist smiling and pulling back the clouds for a minute to reassure the rest of us there's still such a thing as spring.

I was outside breathing steam and breaking ice and chunks o' pavement with a chopper.

Father Naum was in the altar.

Meshes baked by our families were stacked big and round by the table of preparation. The names from each family were listed with each meshe, and one at a time, the old priest added a crumb to the diskos, praying for each person, alive and aloud by name.

Christ, the Lamb of God, Naum set forth in a not-too-large cubelet of bread, in the middle of the little gold diskos, a dish atop a trapezoidal pedestal, Christ the Lamb surrounded by triangular shapes of bread remembering the Holy Mother, the nine ranks of saints and angels, and one for our bishop.

And Naum continued adding a particle of bread for each name, until finally, there it was, on the dish of the golden circle, love made edible: an icon in bread of Saint Alexander the Whirling Dervish Orthodox Church, our little Fishtown parish family, with Christ dwelling in the midst of those of us still struggling this side of the grave, still chopping ice and fighting the good fight, and a particle of bread for those of us out of the body, alive in Christ, those who'd gone before us to their rest, to be with our Savior Jesus, the Eucharist of God.

The list of names and the particles of bread Naum placed on the diskos for each person went on forever. Nicky Zeo said there were hundreds of particles. Little Harry said thousands.

Naum always came early. This was a priest who didn't like to rush. He liked to remember everyone. But not everyone in the community could attend every Sunday, and not everyone who did come had been able to prepare during the week prior the way our mothers taught us to prepare in order to be received into the Communion of Christ's love and life.

On an ordinary Sunday, maybe a hundred people, give or take, had fasted and confessed as directed by their confessor, read the prayers and made an effort to examine their life in Christ and prepare for Holy Communion in our Orthodox way.

Naum never cared to know in advance how many would come. He remembered the Prophet David. He never counted. He said he was afraid of Gad. Not that I knew any Gads in our neighborhood. I guess I shoulda looked Gad up in the Bible when Naum told me it was a Bible thing.

Curtis was an altar server who knew the Liturgy in a way not even Naum could understand. Thirty-five-year-old Curtis knew when to have the censer ready, how to cut the bread for the *nafora*, when to light the candles, how to ready the boys for the processions, when to boil the water for the chalice, even the best way to hold the cloth at Communion time. He carried out every rubric in the book perfectly, but Curtis couldn't read.

The bishop said Curtis was the best server he'd ever seen. "He doesn't have his nose in a book," the bishop said.

Years ago, his mother, Stella, brought him to Naum and said, "My pastor says . . ." And then she hesitated. A generation ago her family had been Orthodox. She wanted to know, "What do the Orthodox say?"

The pastor at her church had told her, "He can't read, so he can't understand, so how can he believe?"

"And if he can't believe—" Stella repeated her pastor's assertion. "How can he be saved, my Curtis?"

Thirty-five years old, our Curtis, and Down syndrome.

Pastor told Stella believers' baptism, for Curtis, was out of the question.

Naum ordered gold baptismal crosses for Stella and Curtis.

Priftereshe Greta adjusted one of Naum's old cassocks for Curtis, and when he put it on for the first time and entered the altar to serve, the look of pure and innocent joy on his face gave the rest of us a preview of what counted for a believer in the Liturgy of heaven.

Little Harry said, "Curtis is a genius over there, in heaven."

At home, Curtis cut pictures from newspapers and magazines, anything that put in his mind an image of church: bottles of wine, men in tall hats or what struck him as religious garb, people lighting candles, round loaves of rustic bread, children singing, caskets and funeral processions, anything that seemed to his eye to resemble a chalice-like cup, an icon, flower arrangements, baskets of eggs, cupolas, steeples, church buildings, and crosses . . . Everyone got a Curtis smile and a bear hug before Liturgy. Everyone received a weekly newspaper clipping from Curtis.

Even though he sometimes sat and dozed off in the altar during the long Lenten evening vigils, he was an icon to us. Curtis even learned to bake the meshe and brought the list of family names his mother had written for the prayers.

Leo Ray Miller came to church the first Sunday after he got out of prison. When he saw Curtis in the altar, Leo said, "Just like the rest o' ya retarded suckers."

We were all afraid of Leo Ray Miller, killed that guy at Henrietta's wedding . . . Little Harry said, "I wanted to tell him, yeah, Leo, Curtis is retarded here, but it's the reverse in heaven."

Course Harry didn't. Why tempt a wounded soul like Leo?

The morning Deacon Donat and his wife Anthia came in, each holding twenty-three-year-old Evdokia by the hand, Anthia said she wasn't sure if it was autism or Asperger's that plagued her sister.

Evdokia, they called her Evie, didn't look any sort o' way— autism, Asperger's, or not. Brown hair. Schoolgirl glasses. Tall and dressed like any other young professional woman on an ordinary church Sunday.

Evie was a brown-haired version of our sunny Anthia. She lit her candles, like Anthia told her, and placed each one in the sandbox on stilts. She watched Diakonia Anthia make the cross and kiss the icons, and Evie did the same.

From behind the *pangar*, the candle counter, Nicky Zeo and Teddy the Horse said, "Hi, Diakonia. Hi, Deacon."

Anthia told them, "This is my sister, Evdokia." She went over and whispered to Nicky, "She's never been baptized. This is her first time coming to church. She's very shy."

Evdokia, loud and aggressive, said, "Are you talking about me? You better not be talking about me."

Teddy the Horse said, "We're gonna go buy doughnuts for after and we just wanted to know what kind you liked."

Evdokia said, "I don't like doughnuts."

Deacon Donat went in to vest.

Anthia and Evie sat in the first pew up front. People were beginning to arrive. The church was filling up.

Madeline came and said hello to the girls in the front pew.

Anthia introduced Evie.

"I'm happy to meet you, sweetie," Madeline said.

"Don't call me sweetie." Evdokia could be touchy. "Why did she call me sweetie?" she said to her sister.

Madeline said, "I'm sorry, Evdokia." She told Anthia, "Lenten potluck after Liturgy. I have five trays of *kukuzeli* in the car." Madeline said, "He was from my town, Durres."

Anthia knew Madeline meant the famous *psalti*, John Koukouzelis, his name meant *beans and peas*. Anthia said, "We'll help you carry them in."

Evie said, "Not me. I didn't say I'd help."

Anthia said, "Okay, Evie. You wait here. I'll be right back." And she went to help Madeline carry the trays.

When she came back, Anthia could hear her sister, Evie, but she couldn't see her.

Her husband, Deacon Donat, was in a panic. He had his head out the deacon's door of the iconostasis, waving Anthia toward him.

Evdokia was inside the altar, and Naum was answering her questions about the diskos and the bread.

The deacons and the men in the altar were gathered 'round listening to the loud inquisitive young woman who'd just pushed the door open and walked in through the south deacon's door.

After Liturgy, as Naum offered the cross to the people and distributed the nafora, we were surprised, sort of, to see Evdokia holding hands with our Curtis, calmly following Madeline to coffee hour in the hall.

When Anthia came to venerate the cross, she said to Naum, "Father, I'm so sorry she burst in like that."

"No worries," Naum told her.

"What did she say in there?

Naum said, "She asked, 'Is this an ordinary Sunday?' I said, yes. Then your sister pointed to the Lamb on the diskos and said, 'You said that little cube of bread will feed all the people who come today?' And I said, yes."

Anthia could see by his face, Naum was still stumbling in wonderment over his encounter with Evdokia.

That day almost a hundred people had communed, and there was more left in the chalice to be consumed after Liturgy.

Naum said, "In all these years, Diakonia, I never thought

about it. I always cut the Lamb the same, a cube, maybe two inches by two. I told her, yes, an ordinary Sunday."

Anthia asked, "Was she trouble, I mean, how did you get her to leave the altar so peacefully?"

Naum had no idea, of course, how stubborn and belligerent Evie could be.

Then Diakonia Anthia stopped and smiled when she realized. She said, "Oh . . . It's okay, Father. I think I understand. We can talk later. There are people waiting to venerate the cross."

It was our Curtis, holding hands with Evdokia, who led her from inside the altar out to the first pew as Liturgy was beginning. She came out with Curtis and sat down next to her sister. She was holding a magazine clipping of a brown-haired girl with glasses, a girl singing in a choir. A girl who looked a lot like her.

Baby in the Womb

F ather." Irene Dinger had asked her husband Bobby to talk to the visiting priest, but Bobby Dinger and his friend Larry Lafferty were busy folding tables and helping with the cleanup after Father Naum's icon presentation at Holy Communion Protestant Church.

Naum was tripping on his cassock, doing the duckwalk toward his car, carrying the big box, when she called him. He turned and saw her. "Irene, right?"

"Father, got a minute?" she said. "I wanted to catch you before you got away."

Irene had been an OR nurse for a long time. When she looked in the mirror she'd tell herself, "Maybe I *could* use some new work clothes." But Irene was so close to retirement, she couldn't bear the thought of buying new scrubs. And the Dansko nurse's shoes she liked were up over a hundred dollars a pair.

Irene called herself a *make-do* woman. She was tall and strong, even as a teenager. Every surgeon wanted Irene right there when they went into the OR.

She made the best damn quiche in the Holy Communion

Undercroft Ladies Auxiliary Group. Five of her recipes were featured in their *New York Times*–reviewed bestselling cookbook.

She could fix a flat, change a washer on a faucet, and not only her husband Bobby but all the cousins in the family said Irene was the center that held the family together.

Her Bobby's hair hardly had a strand of gray. Irene had been coloring hers for more than a few years. The kids were raised. The mortgage was paid, and both the cars were free and clear—old, and maybe the driver's seat was a little sat out in Bobby's car, but free and clear nonetheless. Even Irene's, the one that burned a little oil. Bobby called the fumy tailpipe her James Bond smoke screen.

Holy Communion Protestant had been their church home for two decades, maybe more, but now something was tugging at Irene, something on the inside.

Naum put the big box in the back seat.

"There's no easy way to say this, Father," Irene said, "so I'm just gonna say it. My uncle was an Orthodox bishop." And she named the man. Then she said, "Me, and a couple of the cousins, he molested us." She didn't flinch when she said it. "Boys and girls. On and off over a period of five years."

They stood by the open back door of Naum's car and looked at each other for a long time. The nurse and the old priest, two wounded, limping people. The good nurse could tell Naum had his cross, and she could see the old priest knew suffering when he saw it.

"I've heard of him," Naum said. "Is he dead?"

"Yes," Irene said.

"Good." Naum closed the back door. "I hope he's in hell." He said, "I am sorry for what you've suffered. What must you have carried for all these years? I can't begin to fathom." If Naum could have cried, he would have wept right there.

To his surprise, Irene took his hand to comfort *him*. She said, "It's okay, Father. I'm tougher than I look. The cousins get together a coupla times a year, and we take care of each other. We've learned how to do that. Some of us haven't done so well. Cousin Ronnie drank himself to death, and my sweetie, Myra, my favorite cousin, committed suicide. But most of us are hanging in there. But I don't expect you to do anything about any of that. I know there are good and bad in all the professions, in every church. Only the dead don't have to deal with contradiction. People who do what we do, me and you, we got to learn to live with it, and go on anyway." She looked at Naum and said, "You're the kind that thinks he's got to take care of everybody, aren't you?"

Naum knew there were angels all around the woman whose name meant *peace*. "You saw the angels in the incense tonight, didn't you, Irene?"

That made her smile. She said, "You don't expect me to answer that, do you? What you *can* do for us, what I *do* want to know from you, Father Naum, how do I come back to the Orthodox? Is it possible to go home again?"

———•———

NAUM TOLD PASTOR CALVIN ABOUT IT when they met for breakfast at Betty's.

Calvin stirred his coffee and smiled. "Why did I ever let you give those talks?" he said.

Naum met with Bobby and Irene. He ate supper at their home. At the hospital cafeteria Naum treated Irene and a few coworkers to lunch.

But sitting on the loading dock at the putty factory with Bobby and his work buddy, Larry Lafferty, eating sandwiches, drinking coffee out of a fat steel Thermos? That was Naum's favorite. Swinging his feet over the edge, looking out over the railroad tracks, imagining himself working there with nothing more serious to worry about than what putty got pumped into what can.

Bobby's nephew, Billy John Marco, Catholic kid, was surprised to see the Orthodox priest on the loading dock. "Hey, Father, you did my wedding."

After the wedding fiasco, Naum had called Billy and left a message. He worried the boy's heart would be broken. Who marries a girl and then has her steal the wedding gift money at their reception? The videographer inadvertently caught the whole thing on tape. Billy's bride, redheaded, Orthodox Henrietta, stealing her own wedding money. The marriage was over before it started.

Naum stood to shake the kid's hand. "You're standing up," he said to Billy.

Billy said, "What am I gonna do, Father, lay down and die?"

"I might have," Naum said.

"Nah, Padre, ya wouldn't. My Uncle Bobby always tells me, you Orthodox are tough. He says you people say, 'If you're gonna die, die standing up.'"

Naum admired the faith of Billy John Marco. Been an altar server all his life.

Uncle Bobby had told Naum, "Kid never missed a factory shift, even after what happened. And never misses Mass."

Billy said to Naum, "I got your message. Thanks for caring, just forgot, is all, to call back."

"No worries," Naum said.

"Gotta get back to work, Padre. You remember that other girl from your church, Sunday Stathopoulos?"

"Yes?"

"Date tonight. Gotta do a little overtime. She won't eat no place cheap." Young Billy John Marco, smelling like the chemicals that soaked his gloves and his putty-stained overalls, goggles strapped on his forehead, the industrial filter face mask that didn't do a damn thing around his neck, heading back to finish stripping the residue from the pit, the three-story metallic funnel, told Naum, "Uncle Bobby says him and Aunt Irene like coming to the Saturday night thing at your church."

———

SINCE NAUM'S VISIT TO HOLY COMMUNION, Irene and Bobby were regulars at Vespers. Irene said there was a peace that got inside her. "I never saw my Bobby so engrossed," she said.

Big Bobby claimed he was just tired from all the extra shift work. With the darkened church, the candles, the quiet chant at the lighting of the evening lamps, coulda been Bobby *was* tired, coulda been Vespers too. Either way.

Naum thought it was a shame most folks didn't come for evening prayers. To starve one's soul to such an extent, why?

Icons came alive in the candlelight, and the communion of souls was apparent in the eyes.

The revelation of angels in the incense sealed all doubt in silence by the encompassing comfort of their noetic presence.

Stillness between the phrases of antiphonal chanting recalled each heart to the true homeland of its longing.

The procession of the evening light, the pronouncement of the Church's revelation by the priest, "Christ, our God, He who *is*— is blessed, always now and ever and unto ages of ages . . ."

Sighs too deep for words.

There were no voids.

And the evening and the morning were the first day.

Bobby and Irene, hands joined before the gates of the Garden, like Adam and Eve.

O Great and exalted God, the Only One who is immortal and dwells in unapproachable light; who has created the whole universe in wisdom; who has separated the light from darkness, and has set the sun to rule over the day and the moon and the stars to rule over the night; You have made us sinners worthy once again at this hour to stand in Your presence and offer to You our evening prayer of praise.

Bobby and Irene always stayed in the back. They reminded Naum of two lost kids. They only let go of holding hands to make the sign of the cross.

When the priest and people bowed, Bobby the factory worker and the good nurse Irene did the same. No one had to tell them what they already knew. Bowing down was as much for them as . . .

Naum heard Bobby say, "God don't need us to bow down to Him. We're the ones who need it. Ya gotta know your place, how ya fit in."

Bobby and Irene had been hesitant to tell Naum about the changes at their parish. "We like Pastor Cal, we love him, and all our friends are there, but it's not the same faith as when we started."

"Maybe that's why he invited you to speak to our congregation," Bobby said to Naum. "Pastor Cal ain't dumb. He can read the writing on the wall."

"He's smarter than me," Naum said. "He'd be a great Orthodox."

"Yeah," Bobby said, "but at our age, him too, we all got a pension to protect."

Naum only said, "The faith here ain't gonna change."

Naum pretended he hadn't noticed Bobby and Irene holding hands and weeping together in front of the icon of Saint Matrona the Blind of Moscow.

He told himself, *People often weep when deep calls to deep.*

When Vespers ended they came to venerate the cross. Irene said, "We miss receiving Holy Communion."

"You haven't been going Sundays to Pastor's?" Naum said.

Bobby said, "Hard enough, Father, leaving once."

Naum understood. He said, "Come tomorrow. Come every Sunday if you like. Stay with us for now. It's a safe harbor. Who knows, Bobby, eventually you two lovebirds may even end up embracing the Faith. Either way, you can be here with us. This can be your home for as long as you need it. Like what you told me at break time on the loading dock. 'Sit down and catch your breath.' We'll squeeze you in, make a place. And all the *antidoron*, the blessed holy bread, all you can eat. And Irene, you know better than any of us, a baby in the womb is no less nourished than a baby at the table."

Tough Irene, the make-do woman, she said, "The mother eats, the food is absorbed into the blood, filtered through the placenta, and passes from mother to child through the umbilical cord."

Bobby tapped his head. "Dumb she's not."

Naum catechized best by being taught. He said, "Maybe Vespers is like the umbilical cord, Irene. In the parking lot, you asked me, Is it possible to come home? And here, tonight, holding hands with your Bobby, I think, through your desire for Communion, maybe God has answered you, revealed within the two of you the way He's prepared for you to come home."

Across the Space

———•———

So this is what we heard, us layfolk. Father Naum, the new priest at our Saint Alexander parish, goes to the church hall after Liturgy where all of us are having coffee and talking and smoking cigarettes, and just inside the door there, where they keep the liquor locked up, up over the glass display case where they got a coupla old religious books with the paperback covers curling up at the corners, with icons for sale that've been there from when we was kids, the case where nobody's got the key to open the damn thing and ya got ta jimmy it open, right up there on the wall over the display case, with all the business cards tacked around it, is the phone, and the darn thing starts ringing.

So Naum, he picks it up.

"This is Dennis Donahue, over at Donahue's Funeral. We have a deceased over here, man in his late sixties, name of Thimi Lakuriqui. His wife wants him buried from the church. Looks like he's one of your guys, least from the name. Family wants a viewing tomorrow night, burial the next day. Can you ask the priest if he can do it?"

So Naum, figuring he's the priest and he ain't gotta check with nobody, he goes ahead and says, "Yeah."

Him being the priest and all.

So Naum looks around, every table's packed. Not like Liturgy. And everybody's eating and drinking. Whatever it was that Madeline, and Carol with the big hat, and the Teuta Ladies' Baking Society were cooking, the people were buying it like they hadn't eaten in a week. Especially Ramona's *kurabia* cookies. The smell got everybody so hungry, Bernice had to make another coffee urn, the big one, the hundred-cupper.

Only three ladies on duty that day. Had to get there early. And you know they'll be there late too, those gals. Nobody ever thought to hang around to help with the cleanup.

Things like baptisms, weddings, funerals, having a priest, and the church being there in the first place weren't the only things people took for granted when it came to the parish.

Now the reason why some of the other girls couldn't hang around, see, was 'cause, what they'd do is, they'd put the Sunday roast in the oven before leaving home and hope to high heaven the sermon wasn't too long, 'cause the timing on the Sunday roast was everything, if ya see what I mean, not to mention getting the potatoes and the carrots and whatnot in the pan before all the juices got evaporated. Gotta make a gravy. I mean, what's a Sunday roast without a gravy, for God's sake? Something ta dip the church bread in that the priest gives ya when ya ain't receiving.

And some of these priests, they'd give ya a sermon that could anesthetize an elephant. Nicky Zeo used to make that cutting motion over his throat from the back of the pews, looking at his watch.

He'd tell 'im, "Look, Father, if ya can't say it in seven minutes, ya can't say it." He'd take off his watch, let Naum see him put it to his ear to check it was ticking, shake the damn thing, and roll his finger in the air, like, okay, wrap-time.

Naum would say, "Yeah, I can smell the roasts burning from here."

Anyhow, here goes Naum, walking around the hall asking us about the guy who died. "Thimi Lakuriqui, Carol?"

She looks at him and turns to our Madeline, the parish theologian with the cookie countenance she got famous for 'cause they got the same complexion, Maddy and her cookie namesake. Madeline says, "Don't ring a bell."

Bernice, who's been dressing in lavender ever since Carol got her working part time at her Village Thrift and Consignment, Bernice says, "Nooo. Don't know no Lakuriqui." Making a little laugh 'cause she knows the meaning of the name in our language. Some o' that middle generation could understand it better than they could speak it—Albanian, that is.

Ramona, always with the hippie bandanna, girl looks like she fell through a time warp outta 1965, she don't know him either. None of the women in the Teuta Ladies' Baking Society ever heard of Thimi Lakuriqui.

So Naum goes down the line. Two-Beer Eddie. Teddy the Horse. Nicky Zeo. Lefty. Chicky. Sharky. Vasil Vasili and his wife, Jenny. That whole generation in the middle, guys in their late fifties and early sixties, and the wives—nobody even knows the name.

Course the kids wouldn't know. Not that we have that many kids in the parish anymore. Grew up and joined wherever the ones they married went to church, least that's what we think.

Teddy the Horse, being he sells used cars over at Auto Heaven on the Avenue, he knows everybody. He says, "Father, I even called Sammi over at the store, and Sammi being a local politician and all, he would know. And him and Mikey the mailman, over there drinking raki and coffee, even Mikey don't know this guy, and Mikey delivers to everybody, knows every dog and cat in town. Sammi says youse better go and ask the old guys if any of 'em are around. That's your best bet."

Vasil Vasili, the parish president, said the same thing. "You'd better check with the old ones." Then he told Naum, "And you better hope to hell his dues are paid. If not, the burial fee is higher for a non-member. You don't forget ta tell 'em before you put a pinch o' incense in the burner."

———•———

THE OLD ONES—Antigone and her husband, Misto—were a match marriage in the old country, promised by their fathers when they were infants. When they were married, she was thirteen and he was fifteen. The day of the wedding, the old men in the village told Misto he had to hit his wife. He had to make clear from the beginning his station and her place. The families were outside the newlywed room the first night. They could hear everything.

"It was loud," Misto told Naum.

When they emerged in the morning, the young Misto had two black eyes. She had given him as good as she got. Hundred-and-five-year-old Misto told Naum, "I never hit her again."

Naum thought, *No wonder, she would've killed you.*

Hundred-and-three-year-old Antigone sat crocheting. Naum

asked her, "Nunna, in all your years of marriage, did you ever consider divorce?"

Antigone sat listening to the story she'd heard many times and continued crocheting. A little smile on her face, she said, "I considered murder."

Every week after Liturgy the old couple took home a portion of the antidoron, the blessed bread. Its name means *instead of the gift*. In our language we call it *nafora*. It's rare that any portion of the nafora makes it home. From the time we're children, the homemade nafora is something we all love to eat.

Antigone and Misto kept a portion of the antidoron and made it last throughout the week. Every morning they went to their icon corner. Every morning they prayed. They started each day with a sip of holy water and a nibble of the antidoron, holy bread.

When they could no longer sleep in the same bed for waking each other up, twin beds were pushed close together, a little space between. Misto and Antigone held hands all night across the space.

Now, at 103 and 105, they were Naum's last hope to discover something about Thimi Lakuriqi, the man who had died.

Misto knew the Lakuriqi family. They were from a village in the old country near his own. "Thimi?" He thought for a moment. "*Po*, yes, I remember. He no in the books," the metrical books, in which were recorded the parish baptisms, weddings, and funerals.

Misto said, "He was baptized back there, at home. His father come here, to this town. Work in da rouge room at factory. They got relatives up north. Better job. So they move, New Hampshire, Vermont, one of those, long time ago."

THE NIGHT OF THE VIEWING, Naum goes to the funeral home knowing nothing more than what Misto had told him. He wears his usual funeral getup, the cassock, the *skufia*, the big-sleeved *exorason*, has his bag full of the stuff he needs for the Trisagion Prayers, the memorial prayers. Nobody stands up like we do when we see the priest come in.

Probably didn't bother Naum. He was used to it. The remarks too. Some people laugh at the way our priests look. People laugh at funerals, right?

So Naum goes right up to the casket and venerates Thimi Lakuriqui. He puts a paper icon in the hand of a big man squeezed into a small dark suit.

Dennis Donahue was there. He saw the whole thing. Denny got the business from his father, Dennis Senior. Little Dennis grew up with us. Hung out with Two-Beer Eddie's son, Andon Flynn, who later became a priest.

After, when we saw him, Denny tells us, "So, your priest, Naum, turns and goes over to the family in the first row, he says, 'Mrs. Lakuriqui. Father Naum. Sorry to meet you like this.'"

Dennis says she's a pretty good-looking lady. All dressed in black. Got the hat and everything, even a veil.

Dennis was wondering why they carted this guy from four, five states away, but hey, people come home, right?

Mrs. Lakuriqui doesn't even look up. She barely acknowledges Naum.

Naum asked, "Was it you, Mrs. Lakuriqui, who asked me to come?"

She tells Naum, "He asked me to promise him, on his deathbed."

Turns out it's an older daughter, says real loud to her mother, "Who the hell is this guy?"

Naum said, "I'm Father Naum from your father's church. Tell me your name."

She looks at him in his getup like, *What's it to you, ya weirdo?* and says, "Christina."

Naum said, "If it's okay, Mrs. Lakuriqui, Christina, I'll begin the prayers."

"Who are you, again?" the daughter said.

Naum was blessing the *epitrahilion*. He paused for a minute, holding the stole. "If you like," he said to the daughter, "we can take a minute and go to the room in the back and introduce ourselves. I'm the priest from the Orthodox parish. Your father must have been Orthodox. I guess that's why your mother asked me to come."

The daughter says, "You want all of us, the whole family, to come and talk with you, now?" Ya know she's thinking Naum's got to be mental or something.

Dennis said you could see the irritation spreading to the other family members, but at this point, there wasn't much Naum or Dennis could do.

The daughter says to Naum, "Who the hell is going to be here with my father to greet our visitors if we're all talking with you? My mother's been here all day, what kind of thing is this?" Kid turns to her mother. "Mom?"

Mrs. Lakuriqui stood and turned around to calm the eleven or so family members sitting behind. Then she said to Naum,

"Five minutes? That be enough?"

Naum said, "I'm new at the parish, Mrs. Lakuriqui. I just wanted to learn a little bit about your husband and the family. We can do it another time. I'm sorry if I upset you."

"No," she said. A son-in-law helped her from her seat. "I need a little break anyway."

Denny Donahue escorted Mrs. Lakuriqui, Naum, and a few of the family through his office to the back room.

Yellow wallpaper like on those aluminum butterscotch wrappers. Green-tint glass-top conference table. Bunch of oxblood leather chairs like in a bank, and those bucolic scenes in frames on the wall nobody wants to see anywhere but dentist's offices and funeral homes, the kind with streams and rivers with a perspective that winds away to nowhere.

Denny's there unpacking Naum's bag. Buried all our people, Denny, him and his father, Dennis Senior. Knows our priests too, knows the way we Orthodox do things. Knows how to light the censer, get the candles ready, where to set up the flower arrangements in front of the iconostasis and how to set up the church.

Naum says to the family, "Thanks for talking with me. It will be my voice tomorrow, but your words, your family. He was your husband and father. You know him. You love him."

Naum started with Mrs. Lakuriqui. Others took turns coming in and going out. Naum tried to make a connection. He wanted to learn a little about Thimi Lakuriqui. They weren't saying much.

Born and baptized in the old country.

Came to America as a young child.

Last of the siblings.

Married an American girl from a small town in northern New England.

Two kids.

Worked most of his life in an optical factory.

Not much of a churchgoer.

Twice a year to his wife's church.

Watching sports on TV. That was his church.

A little weekend yard work. 'Bout it.

His baptism was his last time in an Orthodox church, far as they knew. She unfolded an old-world baptismal certificate none of them could read. Beyond the facts, there didn't seem to be much to Thimi Lakuriqui.

In situations where he didn't know the deceased, Naum liked to spend time with the family. It helped to paint a picture of who that person had been, their relationships, the things they considered important, and if, out of a lifetime of blessings, they had ever considered it important to offer anything to others in thanksgiving to God.

It also helped the family to put things in context. Life was spread out on the table, beginning to end, as much as memory would allow.

Naum believed people could see a glimpse of the deceased's love for others in the way they remembered him. It helped to see how much of a man's joy and suffering, consolation and frustration, hunger and satisfaction, had, as Father Alexander Schmemann said, "been referred to their ultimate End, and finally become meaningful."

Under normal circumstances, with a family that was active in the parish, this talk would have taken place a few days before, maybe more than once, usually in the family home. Naum had learned this practice during his time at the cathedral. He had observed Father Agron, always patient and compassionate with those who were suffering, even when they abused him.

The Lakuriqui family didn't seem very cooperative. Denny Donahue said they were the kind of restless that couldn't wait to get the hell out of that room. He could tell they weren't church people.

Denny said, "The one uncle was the only one who talked to Naum for more than a minute. And all he kept saying was, 'One thing about old Thimi, he loved to laugh.'"

When Denny came down to Shooky's Taproom later we told him, "Yeah. We got a buncha people like that. Come to the church only when they need it. They're not used to it. They come once in a while for family stuff, weddings, funerals maybe. They keep looking at their watches.

"Taking time to stop and say thanks? Not these folks. Why? Why would ya? When ya think you're the one it's all from anyway, no benevolent benefactor up there in the great beyond blessing ya, what ya got, *you* provided, right? Why *wouldn't* coming Sunday's ta mouth a meaningless thanks at the ceiling seem like a waste of time?"

Guess Denny'd seen a lot. He said, "They're the type can't wait to get to the food after and have a few laughs. Ya know what I mean. Right? All that God talk and religious stuff makes 'em feel like maybe they gotta stop laughing for a minute and think about when it's all gonna end, and we can't be doing that and still enjoy ourselves, now can we?"

Dennis Donahue, the funeral guy? He's Catholic. He said,

"We all got 'em." Then he said, "The Church has good reason for extending its comfort in death to folks who look for it in life. But then again, the thief on the Cross didn't get it till the last minute, did he? Guess ya can't give up."

Two-Beer Eddie told Dennis, "Yeah, that's why I'm not a priest."

Before Naum and the family went to the back room, Naum told Dennis, "Maybe I was wrong to do this burial in the first place. But I'm in it now, and I don't want to hurt this man's family any further than they're already hurting. Who knows? Maybe some part of the Gospel will reach them—*if* I can avoid putting my foot in God's mouth, or getting them mad at me."

Too late though. Angry words and eyes looking out from a heart full of pain. Christina Lakuriqui was looking for a face to slap. And since she couldn't get to God . . . She needed somebody to receive her indictment of death. She was frustrated with the seeming impotence of the Church. When she let Naum have it and walked out of Donahue's back room, the whole family followed.

Dennis said the priest never got to do the memorial Trisagion Prayers that night at the viewing.

———•———

THEY CAME INTO THE CHURCH early the next morning. It was cold. The family followed behind the casket. It was opened in front of the iconostasis. The paper icon was gone. Thimi Lakuriqui was dressed in a baseball cap and his favorite team's uniform. He was holding a catcher's mitt. Dennis said he'd dressed people in stranger outfits, he just couldn't remember when.

Naum could hear Christina whispering curses at her mother. The faithful daughter wanting to protect her father from this strange part of his past. She chastised her mother for not having services in their home church.

How strange it must have been for them—the incense, the icons, the psalti's atonal chant, the anointing, the few Orthodox, along with Misto and Antigone and some of the elders, standing the entire service while the family sat.

And then when Naum spoke:

In the Name of the Father, and of the Son, and of the Holy Spirit. We have a glimpse of Thimi, through his family.

A family knit together in a time of sorrow. Knit together with love for each other. In their actions they reflect the love they feel for one another, and by this, they reflect the love they have, for husband, father, grandfather, and friend, and the love Thimi had for each of them.

Children surrounding, comforting, protecting, and support-ing their mother. And in what must be so difficult, to bring their father home, to the church of his fathers, so foreign, so strange, home from a far country. It isn't easy, is it? But you loved him so much, you respected his wishes, to come home. This is easy to see, your love and solidarity as a family is easy to see and to understand.

But what is not so easily seen or understood, is why. Why did Thimi Lakuriqui want to come home? What was it that called to him in that final hour?

We know, or so we've been told, he was once in church, in the Orthodox Church, the Church of his fathers, the Church established by our Lord Christ from the time of the apostles. Thimi was in church once, you tell me, only as an infant, to die with Christ and to be raised again with Him, in baptism.

That baptism, no doubt, was nurtured in his mother's home, here in America. We have no doubt, she and her household kept the fasts. Celebrated the feasts. Some of our elders here with us today remember the piety of Thimi's mother, and that of her husband too. Their love of Christ. Their devotion to the Holy Mother. They lived the church year, they kept the fasts and the feasts as best they could, they kept an Orthodox house. Their icon corner, you told me, was kept always lit, a small electric bulb, until they died. Every Saturday night, Thimi's mother, your grandmother, stopped all work. And even though there was no Orthodox church for miles, she prayed as if she were preparing for Holy Communion, and she was. Our future, given to us in the past, says Father Alexander Schmemann, constitutes our present. And your nunna knew this down deep within.

One of you told me Thimi knew the Bible stories from his mother. And that home life, even in a foreign land far away from an Orthodox church, that good father and mother, along with baptism, was like snow that falls on the frozen face of the earth in winter. And when the spring comes, and the leaves sprout on the trees, and the birds return, and the fruit trees blossom, and the flowers bud, when that spring finally comes, no one thinks about the long-ago snow that melted deep within the breast of the earth to bring it all to fruition.

Thimi's Paschal spring, his Passover, was coming. He knew the signs. He had kept the forty days as a boy. His true identity. His true heritage. The memory of the homeland of his heart's

*desire welled up in him as he sensed his time drawing near, and
as a gift to you, his family, he asked you to come and see . . . For
here, preserved in your father's spiritual home, by the grace of the
Holy Spirit, the promise of the Father has been kept unchanged,
in the life of the Only-Begotten Son, here, in your father's church.
And you have come a long way, and overcome much personal
trepidation, putting aside your own understanding in an act of
sacrificial love.*

*It may seem to outward eyes that all Thimi Lakuriqui has
offered to God is the end of life, a body, devoid of life, but our
God is not a God of vengeance. He can make great things grow
from that offered seed. Even seed that has grown old may still
bring forth life.*

He shows mercy upon the last, and cares for the first; and
to the one he gives, and upon the other he bestows gifts.
And he both accepts the deeds, and welcomes the intention,
and honors the acts and praises the offering.

*There's no need for you to wait any further in discovering the
great inheritance God called to the mind of your father at the last
hour. Why not receive it as his final act of love?*

———————

IT WAS YEARS LATER, Naum got a letter, or maybe it was a
phone call, from the Lakuriqui daughter, Christina.

Kid'd found an Orthodox church. Told Naum she attended
Liturgy. Told him she was chrismated, became Orthodox. She
said, "I'm sorry, I didn't understand."

She said, "I found out what our last name means. It means
uncovered, naked, without a garment. I felt that way, till now, I

guess. I just wanted to say how sorry I am."

Naum said, "Understood. No worries. Apology accepted."

———•———

LATER THAT YEAR, Misto died. 105.

Antigone, 103, lay in her twin bed. Helen, her 19-year-old granddaughter, was with her in the bed, to keep Antigone warm.

Antigone lay facing Naum. He sat across the space on Misto's bed. In between was a table with the little church, the Holy Communion kit. The incense was there. The icons in place. She stretched out her hand to Naum and said, "*Urata*, at night, I still reach out across the space to Misto, and we hold hands."

———•———

WHEN CHRISTINA LAKURIQUI CALLED NAUM, he told about it in his sermon, he didn't say who, but we all knew. She called Denny Donahue too, to apologize to him. He's the one told us it was the Lakuriqui kid.

Naum said a young woman whose father died told him, "During the Liturgy, I attend every week now, Father, at my church up here. Every week, my father—at the point where the priest says, 'Help us, save us, have mercy on us, and keep us O God, by Thy grace'—at that point, my father takes my hand. He reaches out across the space, we hold hands, and I go with him, to Communion."

Beautiful in Their Obstinacy

OUT THE WINDOW OF THEIR BEDROOM in the little New England town they could see an ancient farmhouse. Father Naum often dreamed of it. Uneasy dreams. It was a primitive house and boxy, like a barn. It made him close his eyes. He was afraid that if he looked at it too long, it would make him forget the intricate design and complex structures of the neoclassical colonial buildings in the city where he was born. The rough-hewn clapboard beams that ran across its splintered visage made Naum long to run his hand over marble, stone, and brick.

The rows of oblong windows in the old farmhouse opposite the parish house had no shutters. There was never a light over there. Three stories with a black-rust beveled roof. A square, plain white frame that stared back with a vacant gaze, austere and pitiless as Calvin's cursèd earth.

Naum imagined it was the very first shelter raised against these desolate New England winters by the very first Puritan pioneers. He was certain the house had a history of ducking stools and witches' stakes, stone-hearth kitchens, Indian pudding, and plainsong.

At dawn he lay there dreaming of that harsh abode. Dreaming that a barefoot, long-haired woman was sobbing, calling for him, a baby in her arms, scratching on the side door of the parish house.

"Wake up. Wake up." His wife, Greta, was whispering and shaking him. "I hear a baby crying. There's someone at our door."

There in the drifted snow crouched Basilika, her baby close in her naked arms. She huddled tight against the corner of the doorway, hiding from some unseen pursuer in the snow-filled wind.

There was no car. No tire tracks in the driveway or on the empty road. There were no footprints in the snow. Sheer ankle socks on this young mother. No shoes. Her hair was clotted with snow and wild around her face. She wasn't truly a twin, but our people called her the defiant twin. Basilika despised anyone who questioned her. No one could tell her what to do. Dark eyes daring anyone.

Only a thin T-shirt and a diaper on the boy. He had a piercing voice. The network of branches across the blue-gray morning shivered and cracked like pond frost each time he cried out. His tiny feet were raw outside the yellow newborn blanket. The last time they'd seen Basilika was at her wedding.

When Greta reached out to bring them in, Basilika pulled away. "No. You think I'm crazy, don't you?"

"Please, Basi," Greta said, "it's freezing. For the baby's sake. And no, I don't think anything. It's too early."

"And it's too damn cold," Naum said. "C'mon, Basi, bring the baby in, please. We'll have some coffee. And toast."

If Basilika the Headstrong hadn't been so unkempt and coarse, it would've been hard to tell her from her cousin, Tasilika. Old Pandi, their uncle, said, "They're identical opposites."

Unlike the propriety affected by her cousin Tasilika, Basi made no effort to disguise the wild disposition that plagued them both.

Tasi was demure, manipulative, deceptive, and coy.

Basi was brazen, blatant, and in your face.

Tasi was subtle, scheming, and sickeningly ripe with the polished European manner and evasive charm of the generation before.

Basi was Balkan-confrontational and purposely abrupt.

Tasi had stayed at home, remained a virgin, and obeyed her parents' bidding to wait for the right boy, one from our background.

Basi had defied them all and purposely dated and married an outsider.

Naum had been trained at the cathedral and assisted the diocesan chancellor, Father Agron, in more than a hundred weddings, but Basi's marriage was Naum's first time celebrating a wedding on his own.

When he left the cathedral, the little parish of Saint Kosma was his first assignment out of seminary and his first time away from the people of Saint Alexander the Whirling Dervish, his inner-city Philadelphia parish home.

For weeks in advance of Basi's wedding, Naum had tried but failed to get in touch with the monsignor from Notre Dame, the large cathedral in the little New England town. Marc LeClair, Basi's fiancé, was Roman Catholic.

Marc was quiet. Not tall. Apprenticed to the local stonemason and headstone artisan, Marc LeClair was broad and symmetrically muscular as a mastiff. Eyes like faded denim with a glare that made people lower their gaze.

He wept the first time Naum met with the couple in the parish library. Under pressure from his family, Marc suggested to Basi they be married at Notre Dame.

Naum had never witnessed anything like it. Basi was adamant. Mean. Scornful in her refusal. "You wanna be out of my life forever, Marc LeClair?" She told him he'd be "one short, sadly mistaken Canuck."

Marc was motionless in his seat. Tears ran down his face. Repressed anger, sadness, or rage? Naum couldn't tell. He had a feeling this was one incident Basi's man of stone would not forget.

"Look, Father," Marc told the priest, "I haven't been to Mass for years. I couldn't care less. It's my mother, Father. And the Orthodox priest who was here before you, he said at least Monsignor from Notre Dame could come and give a blessing."

The ecumenical courtesy extended to visiting heterodox clergy was spelled out in the *Priest's Handbook* under "Ecumenical Guidelines": Visiting clergy of other confessions may wear a cassock and alb, or a choir gown. No epitrahilion (the stole the priest wears when celebrating the Mysteries of the Church) is permitted.

Father Naum had prepared a seat of honor in front of the iconostasis. At the conclusion of the wedding he would invite Monsignor to offer his personal blessing and congratulations. The chancellor, Father Agron, instructed Naum to tell the monsignor, "Under no circumstances are you to vest or concelebrate."

The Church of Rome was equally clear on the matter. Naum

had checked with the Roman bishop's Ecumenical Liaison Office. To substitute false unity for true communion was no unity at all.

The wedding day weather was straight out of a wedding photographer's dream, clear and blue with just the right kind of clouds, sun enough to make it comfortable for gowns and tuxes and a breeze you'd open the church windows for, without having to worry about it messing with the bride's hair or making the candles drip.

Monsignor still hadn't been in touch. Naum had called, and written, and done everything short of pitching a tent at the cathedral office. If Monsignor's secretary didn't know how to pull that *You again?* face, nobody did.

During his visits to the cathedral office, Father Federico Falatico, who worked the food pantry and soup kitchen, had noticed the Orthodox priest stranded in the waiting room and befriended Naum.

They had breakfast several times. The semiretired Father Fred told Naum, "It's just that he's very busy. But don't worry. If Monsignor doesn't show, I promise I'll be there."

Naum told the choir director at his parish, "I don't blame the monsignor. We have some pretty strict guidelines. They'd discourage anybody. Probably a man of principle, this monsignor. I can respect that."

Naum figured it was probably nothing as grandiose as a dogmatic choice. Monsignor had a large parish. Lots of people to serve, and only one semiretired priest to assist him.

"Guy has better things to do," the choir director said. "We have one hundred and fifty people. He has fifteen hundred families. How often does this kid she's marrying attend Mass over there?"

Father Naum said, "I get it. Still, my heart goes out to Marc. Dealing with what he's dealing with? Probably easier moving granite at the quarry."

Crowds of wedding-dressed guests, limos, and flower delivery trucks were out front, and the church was already filling up when Naum ducked out the back door of the parish house and slipped across the lawn and into the church through the side door.

Good cousin Tasilika, the decorous twin, had white flower arrangements decorating the aisle end of every pew. Photographers were checking light meters and camera angles, arranging tripods, and setting up what was becoming standard at every wedding, video recorders.

The wedding table was centered in front of the iconostasis. It was covered with a special white cloth Basi's family had brought from the old country. In the center of the table sat a silver tray. The tray held the holy bread, the prosphora, the bread our people call the meshe. Rice and brightly colored candy-coated almonds, representing the bitter and sweet of marriage, were strewn around the bottom of the tray.

The long white wedding candles sat one on each side of the gold-covered book of the Gospels, and the wedding crowns, formed from two laurel wreaths connected by a single white ribbon, angled at opposite corners atop the Gospels.

The blessing cross, the common cup covered with a red cloth, the basil sprig tilted in the crystal bowl of holy water, and the cut-glass flask of wine were on the table. The golden censer swayed to a halt on its stand. Everything perfectly asymmetrically in place under the icon of the Wedding at Cana, the wedding we knew to be that of Simon the Zealot.

The groomsmen and the bridesmaids were all rehearsed. Each step along the wide white runner, each duty, and where each person was to stand had been carefully prepared.

When Naum entered the side door of the church, Monsignor Cauvin was standing in the room off the altar, fully vested in what looked like the poncho of a Peruvian alpaca herdsman high in the Andes.

He smiled and said, "Hurry, Father, we've got a wedding to perform."

Father Falatico, in his black suit and clergy shirt, was waiting there too. He would have apologized to Naum with more than his eyes if he could have done it without causing undue commotion.

Groomsmen were milling around the room. Marc LeClair sat in his chair. Naum took Monsignor by the wrist and said, "Ya ever seen our library?"

The two of them did the quickstep across the front of the crowded church with Falatico close behind.

Naum noticed Basi, her father, her cousin Tasi, and the bridesmaids at the head of the center aisle silhouetted in the light of the open front doors.

Monsignor didn't have a chance to say much. Next thing he knew, the three priests were locked in the library.

"You know the deal, Monsignor," Naum said.

"Now let me stop you right there, mister." Tall, red-faced, handsome Monsignor Jackie Cauvin. Naum couldn't believe the guy still had a full head of thick white hair and a smile that'd charm the gargoyles right off of his own Notre Dame Cathedral. Monsignor said, "I called our liaison officer with the Orthodox when I received your letter informing me of what I could and could not do at this service."

Falatico stood behind him shaking his head.

Naum wasn't sure if it was the clean shave or the chilled blue eyes, but he had to give Monsignor credit. Dude was cool.

"Let's get one thing straight, buster." His tone was quiet but firm. "I. Am. The priest in charge." He took a minute to tap the table. "Senior in this town. From *the* church. *The* cathedral parish of this town. It says Orthodox Catholic over the door of your parish, doesn't it? You're Catholic. Our sacraments are the same. Vatican Two. So let's just agree that *you* will assist me, the senior priest."

Naum said, "Monsignor, you *are* the senior priest, to your people, at the cathedral. I respect that, but here? Different story."

"I insist"—he interrupted—"that you conduct yourself, for the sake of this young couple, with a little decorum. A little compassion. A little Christian charity. *I thought* a *married* priest would understand the dynamics here a little better. Marc's in between a rock and a hard place."

Naum could see Monsignor downshifting now into pastoral mode. He extended his hand. "Now, c'mon. Let's make this a beautiful wedding for these kids." An unmistakably authoritative gleam of mischief in his placid blue eyes.

Naum knew Basi was out there pacing. Any minute she'd be putting Marc up to crunching through the door. He dialed Father Argon at the Diocesan Office.

"What are you doing?" Monsignor said.

"Calling Father Argon, our chancellor," Naum told him.

"I already spoke with him about all this yesterday. I don't mean to embarrass you, but he was the one apologizing. Look,

Father, you know there's the letter of the law, and how we balance it with a given pastoral situation. Which is what we have here. Your chancellor is on your side. He explained this was your first time doing a wedding on your own. He gave his approval for my taking the lead and you assisting me, to help you, to help these kids."

Monsignor tried the door, but it was locked, and Naum had the key in his cassock. Monsignor said, "Let's go. The bride is waiting."

The line was busy. Again and again. Naum put an emergency call through to the operator.

Monsignor reached for the phone. "Give me that damn phone. This is ridiculous."

Father Fred couldn't believe what he was seeing. He said, "Please, fellas . . ."

Monsignor looked his way, and Father Fred went back to perusing the library's Patristics shelf.

Naum was afraid. Most of the Roman clergy he'd met to this point were heroes. Serving the poor. Teaching. Working in hospitals. Living in the ghettos. Establishing universities. Standing up for the rights of the unborn. Even regular guys serving parishes, in Naum's experience, had been gentlemen all the way down the line. In spite of himself, Naum couldn't help but love this guy. Monsignor was a trip.

Father Agron was greeting the casket at the door of our cathedral. Everything came to a stop. "No, I did not speak with the monsignor," he said to Naum. "Put him on the line."

Monsignor's face, and then his shoulders, flattened to a semitone, like our choir trying to learn a new hymn.

In the end, when Monsignor hung up with Father Agron, Naum thought, *All in all, this monsignor is one cool customer.*

He took off his vestments, said to Naum, "Good man, that Agron. Wish I had him at my back."

He walked to the seat of honor and sat there satisfied, grinning like a guy who, even though he lost, had still ended up just where he wanted to be.

After, when Naum invited him, he came forward and gave his personal blessing and congratulations to the couple on behalf of the cathedral community.

Father Falatico stood in the pews and from there sang along with the choir. Naum knew Falatico loved icons. He was surprised Father Fred seemed to know the Orthodox hymns.

Later at the reception Naum said, "Thanks, Monsignor, I was about to be nervous doing my first wedding on my own, but you took care of that."

"Think nothing of it, dear boy," he said. "I was impressed by your composure under fire. Now your singing voice? That's another matter. You're no Pavarotti."

Naum could tell Monsignor'd had a few.

"Let's drink a toast to your chancellor," Monsignor said. "Guy has gusto. Doesn't mince words, does he? French's pretty good too. He said he was sure you'd do the right thing and share the honorarium." That got a wink. "And, while we're at it, here's to your Basilika. What resolve. Her insistence on being married in your little chapel when she could've had the cathedral. They're like you Orthodox priests, aren't they, your women? Beautiful in their obstinacy."

THE SKY WAS GETTING LIGHT. Snow was still falling. They sat in the kitchen. The baby was asleep where they could see him on the sofa. Basi was wearing one of Greta's old robes and a pair of heavy socks. She had a towel around her head.

Naum was making another round of toast. Greta was pouring more tea. She said, "The baby eat the oatmeal, Bas?"

"He loved it. Thank you, Priftereshe. Your boys must still be asleep?"

"You kidding? On Saturday morning? If it wasn't for cartoons they'd sleep till noon." It was 6:45 on the kitchen clock. "Be up in an hour or so," Priftereshe Greta said.

Now that it was getting light, they could all see the ancient farmhouse across the road. The primitive boxy house. The one that gave Naum uneasy dreams. The one that made him long for the neoclassical colonial buildings and cobblestone streets in the city of his birth.

They could see its many rows of shutterless, oblong windows. No light over there. The black-rust beveled roof. The square, plain white frame with the vacant gaze. Austere and pitiless. Ducking stools and witches' stakes, stone-hearth kitchens, Indian pudding, and plainsong. No one spoke.

After a while Basi talked about her husband.

Marc had left the stoneyard. He had a new job on the overnight shift at the local aircraft factory. He talked in his sleep about sabotaging helicopters. He told her he was dancing with the devil on a narrow ledge. He was harsh with her and aggressive with everyone. He wore headphones all the time. She could hear the music. It was loud and assaultive. She found drugs in the house. He'd lost interest in sex, in food, in the baby, in life.

She was frightened of her child's strange faces and of the sounds the baby made when he awoke in the middle of the night, and her inability to comfort him, she said, just freaked her out.

Marc never held the boy and went berserk if she mentioned baptism. One night she found him standing over the crib with a hammer in his hand.

Marc was in their kitchen when Naum took Basi and the baby home that morning. All the kitchen knives were lined up on the table. He was polishing them.

Marc agreed to go with Naum to see their family doctor. Father Falatico agreed to meet them there.

———·———

THE HAMLETS AND TOWNS of western New England reminded Naum of the Currier and Ives Christmas villages he'd seen as a boy in department store windows.

Spindle-grim spires pointed accusatory steeples at the guilty gray sky and kept a joy-dampening eye on the festive tour-bus happiness at the craftwork shops spread under the wide white oaks along the brick-patterned sidewalks of the cobbled Main Street.

A rocky winding river flowed fast and brown under a coal-black trestle. The far-off echo of an unseen train signaled unscheduled stops in the middle of a night that unnerved Naum and sent him to his knees in the space where two dark walls dead-ended in the single-candle portal of his wordless icon corner.

Walking home from funerals along the slate-topped spine of

the stumble-stone wall, Naum often bent to take paper-rubbings from tilted marble headstones indecipherably thin and layered in moss more than two centuries thick. Hidden habitations where colonial mothers and forefathers slept among peacefully treed hillocks and broad bucolic mounds.

And from everywhere in the little town, her pleasant countenance blessed the people, monumental on the high ground and royal in the midst: Monsignor's Cathedral of Notre Dame. Every mill town's envy. A chunk of heaven alighted in the rolling panorama of the Berkshires. Marble shiny and divinity bright. Staid, yet stuck in her place, as separate from the rest as she was hopelessly hemmed in by the bracelets and hoops of our low surrounding hills.

An otherworldly gemstone set in a collage of harvest foliage like Naum had never seen. Terraced, rising elevations crowded with columns of white spruce, gray birch, scarlet oak, and eastern black walnut, all dressed in colors so sublime his eyes wept in their effort to describe them to his brain.

He never understood how that very same landscape in winter could shrivel to a scene so threadbare and barren that it made his soul shiver. And on endless winter mornings he'd find himself wakened by a frigid stillness with Greta saying, "Who knew snow could be deafening?"

Every tree limb, every housetop, each wisp-curling chimney, all muffled overnight in the silence of a slow-falling snow.

Smoky gray ghosts long buried in each family woodpile escaped up smokestacks and spewed splintered, bitter sparks through the dense snowy darkness.

Burrowed under heavy cross-knit cable covers she made in

the autumn, Priftereshe and Naum watched the drifting descent of each firework cinder, ignited and cremated and consigned to oblivion.

Reflected on the windows, burnt-orange embers filled the room with the smell of wet corroded metal and hissed with steam as they pierced steeples and cupolas and bent rooftop stovepipes and sifted ashes of regret like unconfessed sin over each lonely shed.

———

ALL WINTER LONG Naum's family bundled around the fireplace and the wood-burning stove in the kitchen, listened to the radio, danced the limbo, and ate chocolate-covered cherries, encouraging one another in hope for the long longed-for spring.

Then New England's short little growing season and summer flitted by across the parish house window like a swift-flying robin come and gone out the corner of the eye.

Secluded Saint Kosma, the little Orthodox church, stood alone on the edge of town, straddling the last paved road and the stony, hidden stream where in the evening Naum and his family watched the deer come to drink.

That summer, before he and his family returned to Saint Alexander the Whirling Dervish and their inner-city hometown Philadelphia neighborhood, Naum went to the farmhouse with the incense and holy water.

Basi said he exorcised it.

Naum said the room where Marc used to isolate himself was unseasonably cold. Marc asked him to bless it three times.

The little boy was baptized at home. Both families were there and sang the responses. Father Falatico too. They ate. It was a sweet thing. Marc went back to the quarry. Things got better.

That's all Naum would ever say.

Coming Attractions

———•———

SAMMI'S SPA IS A NEIGHBORHOOD lunch counter/conve-
nience store. Why they called it a spa, who knows? Some
people say all the waitresses are ex-felons, the silverware's dirty,
and the cook ain't washed his hands since Thanksgiving. But
that's what people in the neighborhood grew up calling Sammi's
mini-grocery lunch counter. A spa.

Sammi Leka, who owns the place, is a member of Saint Alexander the Whirling Dervish, Naum's church. He's a local com-
mitteeman, Sammi, a Philly political ward leader.

We'd all see him, there on local cable TV, debating some issue
with a cigarette in his hand, waving his arms around like he was
chasing black flies with a punk stick. Most people watched with
the sound down just for a laugh.

Tell ya what, though, when it comes to bobbing and weaving
in the neighborhood, Sammi gets it done. A parking ticket. A
zoning variance. Your kid got in trouble with the law throwing
snowballs at cats, or got drafted. Somebody needing a job or is
out of work and needing a basket and a couple of bucks to tide 'em
over, or got so drunk down at Shooky's Taproom they couldn't

find their way home and ended up sleeping on some other lady's couch and caught a charge? Sammi's the man.

Sammi pulled a lot of weight at church too. He did it through whichever one of the Black Bridge boys was sitting on the parish council that term. Sammi never attended church, mind you, he said he had his reasons, but he grew up with the whole crew. Lefty. Two-Beer Eddie. Chicky. Sharky. Nicky Zeo. Teddy the Horse. Went to war with 'em too.

Father Naum used to tell Sammi, "You can't come to the church, so the church will come to you." And the old priest would visit Saturdays at the Spa once or twice every month.

Sammi loved to see Naum come through the door.

Father Naum would always put on the same act. "Sammi, I really don't like you, or our talks, or debating theology with a politician. But this old-fashioned lunch counter, the marble-top soda fountain, the stools, the big mirror, and your father's old grocery store next door, that's why I come. And Celine's tuna sandwich with the side of potato salad and some chips. How *you* got *her* for a wife? I'd be fat as a bishop if I had a wife like Celine. And that's precisely why I don't come more than I do."

Sammi hated Saturdays. George, his father, the old neighborhood huckster who used to go around with a horse and wagon, he died on a Saturday. Sammi's mother, Evdokia, too, and his younger sister, Amelia.

Naum's Saturday visits took Sammi's mind to another place.

One cold October Saturday morning as he was opening the Spa, Sammi had a heart attack, a serious heart attack.

When Naum arrived at the hospital, Sammi was sitting upright in bed, his thin wiry frame propped against pinstriped blue pillows and waffle-weave blankets colored dull moody beige, tubes and lines running over and under the blankets in an untraceable maze.

Sammi's face was the bland color of Cream of Wheat. The stubble on his chin made his lips and his whole face look razor-blade blue.

The monitors beeped lightning azure lines across a digital dark-sky screen like metronomic birds chirping in an LED cage. A winking synchronicity moved the surface of the sleeping councilor's closed eyes. The arrhythmic burble of his breathing rattled in the bellows of the machine that pumped the oxygen. The dismal pale yellow and the smell of the iodoform gauze made it all that much more apparent: the futility of our fight for life, the icon of our fragility, stretched out in the bed. It frightened our poor Naum to the point where he dared not disturb his wounded friend.

Sammi's thick gray hair stuck out in every direction like the metal scouring pads in the Spa's commercial kitchen. Under the drooping hospital gown, Naum could see bloodied stitches that ran like railroad ties along the incision down the center of Sammi's chest.

Naum didn't want to wake him. He blessed the epitrahilion and put the stole quietly around his neck, whispering in Sammi's first language the Trisagion Prayers.

O Heavenly King, Comforter, Spirit of truth, who are everywhere present and filling all things . . .

At the Lord's Prayer, closed-eye Sammi began to chant along with Naum. Then his eyes opened. He was staring past the priest, seeing or hearing something or someone the priest couldn't see or hear. It unnerved Naum.

Naum took Sammi's hand in his. He brushed back his hair and kissed his head. He covered Sammi's head with the stole, the epitrahilion.

"O Almighty God, who casts down and lifts up again; by whose wounds we have received healing; who strikes and again bandages up: we thank You that You have not seen fit to give your servant, Samuel, over to death . . . Grant that the chastisement of his body may purify his soul . . ."

Sammi said nothing as Father anointed him. He just looked and nodded. Sammi this calm? Naum had never seen it.

"I don't want you worrying about anything, Sammi," Naum said. "We've been to the house. Celine, all your family, you know they were here, right? The kids? God has his hand on you, no doubt. You're gonna bounce back quick."

———

OUR PEOPLE HAD A SAYING: *If you're gonna die, die standing up.* Much as Sammi's wife, Celine, complained that he should get some rest, it didn't stop Sammi. Two weeks later he was hobbling into the Spa. Naum caught him early that first Saturday morning going in through the back of the old grocery store next door.

The dark wood paneling was colored by muted daylight filtering through old-fashioned red- and gold-trimmed lettering—GEORGE'S GROCERY AND DRY GOODS—faded now by sun and years.

"*Ti je?*" Naum said. "How are you?"

"*Mire.* Good," Sammy said. "For a minute there, Urata [he who blesses me, the way our people address a priest] . . . for a minute there, I was in the coming attractions over at Wackerman's

Funeral Home, but here I am."

The old grocery store, no longer open to the public, was used as a storage area and an office for Sammi's Spa and his political electioneering. Posters, and placards, and patriotic bunting—enough to paper a metropolis, let alone our small Fishtown neighborhood ward.

Sturdy wooden shelving
Climbed the walls
From the plank-board floors
To the stamped tin-plate ceiling
Arcade video games and pinball machines
Furniture from Sammi's defunct motel, the Pink Flamingo
His father's horse-drawn wagon—wooden wheels and all
Bowling alley equipment from another failed venture
Celine had exiled every failed scheme to the old grocery store
Junk elbowed junk into every corner
Snatches of Sammi's ambition
Scrambled to the top in teetering piles
The fixtures and enameled signs from the grocery store
Stood waiting in place
Glass-topped display cases
White enamel meat scales and shiny bladed slicers
Fruit stands, boxes and bins
Vegetable crates bright with colorful field art label-ends
A tall brass register majestic as a waxed handlebar mustache
All ready and waiting for a grocer's long day
The black wood hat rack stretched accordion-like open
Across the wall behind the counter

Ivory buttons capping each lathe-spindled peg
A once-taut wire sagged the length of a grip-worn pole
A squeeze handle at the bottom opened and closed
A two-finger grabber at the slim far end
Reaching top-shelf dry goods, jars full of jam, Quaker Rolled
White Oats, and the penny candy thievery of little boys' necks
Its forlorn claw now dangled on a hat-rack peg
Next to a faded butcher's apron stained with 1950s time
A shiny metal produce scale hung suspended midair
Weightless in space—its Detecto needle stuck on zero-red
And timeless Luzianne hung high on the wall behind the
motionless hands of her unplugged clock and promised with a
smile that her coffee and chicory were both robust and rich
The harness that once bridled Me-Fat the horse
Now saddled some pegs on the wall over the wagon
It grew more dusty and encrusted
Than old man George and Me-Fat the horse
Could have hoped for on the driest day of August
In busy summer, hucksters now long shouted out and gone

When they entered the Spa, a mailman's brown leather satchel was sitting in the sunlight just inside the door. The look and the smell of the leather reminded Naum of the tack room in the stable where he used to groom horses as a boy.

Sammi unlocked the front door. He turned on the lights. Put on the coffee pot, picked up the TV remote and hit *On*. Then he took his regular perch on the stool under the television, which sat on a shelf in the corner above the lunch counter.

He had a cigarette in his hand. His wire-haired terrier, Kenny, nuzzled at his feet. "Sit," he said to Naum, and Kenny obeyed.

The door opened, and Mikey the mailman came in. "I knew I left that somewhere for a reason," he said, happy to see his satchel.

The mailman went behind the counter and poured three cups of coffee into those brown plastic holders for white disposable pointed-bottom plastic cups.

"Mikey. I want you to meet my priest," Sammi said.

The mailman plopped onto the next stool, swung his heavy black shoes toward Naum and put out his hand. "I heard about you," he said. He sipped the coffee. "Ah, good."

"Yeah, Mike, the one I was tellin' ya about," Sammi said.

Nobody ever watched the damn TV, but Sammi put it on for background noise anyway. "The yack distracts me from thinking about you know what." And he touched his chest.

Naum wanted to tell Sammi—maybe not in front of Mikey the mailman, but he wanted to tell him. He said, "You remember the passage I wrote out for you, Sammi? When you were finally eating solid food again in the hospital?"

"You know, it wasn't that bad, the hospital food." Sammi crushed his cigarette in a green aluminum ashtray. "Yeah, I got it right here." He took the folded sheet from his pocket. "And I read it. And I get your meaning, about the day drawing near."

Therefore, brothers, since we have confidence to enter the holy places by the blood of Jesus . . .
Let us draw near with a true heart . . .
Not neglecting to meet together, as is the habit of some, but encouraging one another, and all the more as you see the Day drawing near . . .

"And, I didn't forget, you saying the great priest over the house of God is not you, right? I forgot some stuff since the, ah, incident, but not that, or what you're trying to get at with the note. I get it. Okay? Me, coming to church. Right?"

Naum waited.

"But, Father," Sammi said, "it's like this." And he winked at Mikey. "If I'm at church on Sunday morning, then my mind, ya see, is here at the store. So, of course, if I stay here . . ." Sammi made a grand sweeping motion that encompassed all the bright, colorful cans, jars, and boxes stacked and positioned, every label precisely aligned and edged on the shelves, to the ice-cream freezers, the coolers full of milk and soda, the penny-candy counters with the shiny glass cases, the magazine racks, the piles of newspapers by the door. "If I stay here, Father, well."

Naum was watching Sammi's eyes. He was staring at the old photographs of his father, his mother and sister, the first dollar, the framed mercantile license, and up in the corner above the TV, the icons of the Holy Mother, Samuel the Prophet, and Saint George.

Sammi nodded his head and bit his bottom lip. "You came and gave me the *Kungo* . . ."

I will bless the Lord at all times . . . I sought the Lord, and He answered me . . . This poor man cried, and the Lord heard him, and saved him out of fear and trouble . . . Oh, taste and see that the Lord is good!

"This poor man cried," Sammi said, touching his heart, "and the Lord heard me. He knows, Father, if I stay here, well, then, my mind's at the church. I think you get what I'm saying."

Mikey was the only one drinking his coffee. "Can't argue with that logic," he said. "You're here, ya think about the church. At church, ya sit there in the pew and worry about getting back here."

Sammi and the priest knew why they'd kept the fast, why neither had touched the coffee.

"Sam, gotta get back to work." The mailman shouldered his leather pouch. He waved through the plate glass and disappeared down Hancock Street.

"Urata, I saw something there, at the hospital. I wasn't worried, like you thought. I only told Kenny. Right, Kenny?"

The dog looked up. *Qeni* was our word for "dog." Sammi reached for the remote and muted the TV.

BBC News was broadcasting a live feed. A well-known, old-time Protestant evangelist from the States was preaching to a packed house inside an Orthodox Church in Russia, where the people had embraced the Gospel in the year 988.

Naum could see by the captions scrolling across the bottom of the screen, the self-styled prophet and evangelist was telling the people about Phoebe Palmer, the nineteenth-century founder of the Holiness Movement, and that they needed to repent and become Christians.

Mitered bishops and vested priests sat in rows along the iconostasis. Naum wondered, *Ubi pastoribus ad ipsos? What sorrow awaits the leaders of my people—the shepherds of my sheep—for they have destroyed and scattered the very ones they were expected to care for, says the LORD.*

Sammi caught Naum's attention. "They were there, at the foot of my bed."

He spoke in a sober, even tone. Naum had never seen old Sammi so serious or sincere.

"I'm making the cross, Urata. They were calling me, with their ugly fingers. Not even in France, in the war, not even then. I was more scared with them at the foot of my bed, there's no way to tell it."

Naum knew Sammi was one of the neighborhood boys who'd survived D-Day at Normandy.

"I felt a hand on my right shoulder, behind me. *Krishti*." Christ. Naum made the cross and said, "Krishti."

"I can't describe, Urata," Sammi said. "Like a boy whose big brother appears out of nowhere and saves him from bullies in the schoolyard." His eyes filled up behind his half-rimmed black glasses, but his smile never changed.

"Can you believe it?" he said. "Me, worm of the earth. You don't know what we did over there. How could I ever go into a church after what they had us do, go in the door even? And you know what He says, Krishti? With His hand on my shoulder. To them? He looks at them and says, 'This one's with me.' I tell ya right now, Urata, my mother and father are my witnesses, my sister Amelia, too.

"I wanted to go with Him right there and then. I didn't care for nothing. I wasn't worried about nothing, and I looked down, and they were gone, the ugly ones were gone, and there you were, standing there, praying."

Naum unpacked the Communion kit his mother had given him when he was ordained. The mini-church, eight inches high, four inches wide, and three inches deep, plated in gold and topped with a Byzantine cross. A long gold chain was attached on either side of the golden box. The door opened in the front.

Naum took a small chalice from an interior recess and a spoon from a special holder on the inside back of the door. He removed a small lidded box from above the chalice recess. It contained the bread of the Holy Communion. A small vial from another recess contained the wine. Another vial held the anointing oil. He spread a red cloth on the marble lunch counter. The charcoal for the small hand censer was lit. A candle too.

"Put in a piece of *temjan,* one for each of your family," Naum said to Sammi, and he placed the nuggets of frankincense in Sammi's hand. "And get your family icons from the shelf."

Sammi asked, "Lock the door?"

Naum said, "No."

The hand cross was on one side, the Gospel book on the other. He opened the priest's *Book of Needs,* blessed the epitrahilion, and placed it around his neck. *The one thing that was needed* was placed in the chalice, warm water was added with the wine, and together, the two men prayed.

For where two or three are gathered in My name, there am I among them.

"Really, Urata," Sammi said, "I still can't believe it. Sometimes I sit here and think about it. My picture really was in the coming attractions over at Wackerman's Funeral. I look at the pictures on the wall up there, like icons, my mom and pop, my sister, up there with the real icons.

"I say, 'Pop, Mom, Sissy, I just pray Krishti came for you too.' I know you were with them too, Naum, when it was their time, at the end. It was like you gave me a passport, like I came alive when you put that in my mouth there at the hospital, like *He* gave me a passport. You know what I mean. He was there Himself, He is the passport, and He sent you too, I guess. I can't understand it. I guess I don't have to. But whatever He did in me, Saturday ain't the same dead end it used to be."

Naum could hear himself not talking.

Sammi looked at Naum and said, "Thank God some of our boys answered the right door when He knocked. Some of us just followed a whole different gang to a whole different end. I ain't gonna lie and say it couldn't've been me."

Naum was packing the little church.

"You gonna come every Saturday now, right?" Sammi said.

"Depends on what's for lunch," Naum said.

The confectioned fragrance escaped when Sammi lifted the glass dome off the cake stand on the silver pedestal and said, "Here, have a doughnut. Ya can dunk if ya want. They're good for ya, like vitamins. Just don't tell Celine. She thinks ya come here for her tuna hoagies and potato salad."

Catechized Best

———◆———

NAVY CHAPLAIN PASTOR CALVIN HALL was used to Laney being the center of attention at his weekly Twelve Step drug and alcohol group. She made the time blow by like clouds over the flight deck on a windy day. He figured if there was one intentional omission on everybody's Step Four inventory—*making a searching and fearless moral inventory of ourselves*—it was probably the happy distraction of Laney's figure and the way she dressed.

Cal didn't count his own searching inventory to be fearless or immune where Laney was concerned. Every time she crossed her legs he had to close his eyes and start over again.

He was no different from any other man, but he'd read *The Unseen Warfare*. He had no doubt he was the gunpowder and Laney was the match, and he'd go home and read it again after every group.

It's not her, he told himself, *it's me.* He knew that. He had a wife and two daughters. *It's my problem. My longing. My fire. Laney's just Laney.*

Laney wasn't working out of any book. Laney *was* just Laney. Not unlike Potiphar's wife with Joseph. She cornered Cal after group session and got close enough to see the reflection of her flame in the chaplain's eyes, close enough to tell she was having the desired effect. Laney, the wife of a fellow naval officer, told the pastor, "Oh c'mon, Cal, don't go getting your signal flag tangled in the halyard. This session could be something we'll remember for a long time."

Pastor Cal may have borne in mind his commissioned priority, *promote ethical and moral behavior throughout the Sea Services*, but probably took the wrong tack with Laney when he told her, "Maybe your addiction's not so much to drink, Laney, as it is to being told *yes*."

"Really." Laney backed off a step, but still close enough for her breath to turn into a kiss on their lips, and when he didn't breathe back, she put a finger to his chest. "Well, Calvin, we all know your addiction, you *and* your God, telling people *no*. You get off on that, don't you, Calvin? Well, I promise you one thing, Lieutenant *JG*"—digging in the "Junior Grade" to sting—"*this* is one session you're not going to forget for a long, long time."

Both her husband's report to the commanding officer on Navy Chaplain Lieutenant Calvin Hall and the chaplain's defense were classic *she said–he said*.

Cal tried to reason it out, but it seemed the more he defended himself, the guiltier he got. He wanted to be angry. But he couldn't sustain it. His own family didn't seem to know him beyond the so-called facts. He could see it in their eyes when he said he was innocent. Innocent or no, Laney's accusation cut like a razor.

And it damn sure left a scar Cal swore people could see, like a diagonal tattoo etched across his face. Everybody seemed to look at him sideways. He dogged himself. Trepidation and self-doubt furrowed a scar so long and deep in his soul that this side of the grave he knew nothing would ever grow there, and the wound would never heal.

Laney herself refused to make a statement in open court—said she was too traumatized, said it would just revictimize her.

When it came to the hearing, Cal was a high school batter standing at the plate, facing a major-league pitcher. Laney's husband was an attorney assigned to the Judge Advocate Corps, and Laney was no stranger to the Navy policy on sexual harassment. The colleague who stood in for Laney's husband had never lost a case. He pitched a perfect game.

"It all just made me look like the dumbass I was." Pastor Calvin barely got out with an honorable discharge.

THE PATRIARCH JOSEPH did two years' prison time when he was falsely accused by the wife of Potiphar. Sobriety didn't catch up with Laney till thirty years later, when she finally recanted her charges against Pastor Cal.

Her venomous accusations had brought the gavel down on his life: Three decades, I sentence you, Lieutenant JG, Pastor Calvin, Chaplain *Hard-Time Hall*.

Cal used to say, "It was a slow-acting poison."

The thirty-year necrosis Laney introduced putrefied the fabric of Pastor Cal's life like a spider vein of mold spreading through a big wheel of pecorino. His wife left him. His daughters thought all men were predatory creeps, and the life they had at home may as well never have been.

Hard-Time Calvin Hall lived a solitary life in an empty parish house by himself.

Only people who didn't know about Laney and her allegations believed a word that came out of Cal's mouth. The man was pretty much marooned on his own island.

The only thing he hadn't lost was some sense of hope. "And that's a miracle in itself." He'd tell himself and anyone who would listen, "She drank the poison, and me and mine are the ones who wasted away."

Cal wasn't an addict, never had been, but he'd known some in his time. He'd accompanied friends, colleagues, and clients to *the rooms*, to AA and NA meetings, many a time, day and night. He'd conducted more groups and heard more variations on the same sad story and then some, more broken-life renditions than he cared to recall.

It got to the point where he told the old joke but no longer found it funny: "What's the difference between an alcoholic and an addict? An alcoholic will steal your wallet and lie to you. A drug addict will steal your wallet and then help you look for it."

———•———

ONE DAY CAL GOT A CALL FROM LANEY. He was surprised he recognized her voice.

"I'm on Step Eight and Nine in my recovery," she told him.

Something in him wouldn't let him be mean. "Eight and Nine. Good for you, Laney."

Laney's call had him looking over his shoulder. He wondered if she could tell her call frightened him.

She told him she'd made a list of all persons she'd harmed, and that she'd become willing to make amends to them all.

"I'm making direct amends to such people wherever possible, except when to do so would injure them or others." She was quiet for a moment, and then she said, "I've injured you, Cal, haven't I?"

Cal knew he had to get off the line. "Don't worry about it." He said, "Please let me excuse myself, and good luck to you, Laney."

———

PASTOR CAL WAS SERVING the Holy Communion Protestant congregation in our Fishtown neighborhood. He met our priest, Naum, at the annual Ecumenical Clergy Association Thanksgiving service. Now for the first time in a long time, tall, blond-haired Calvin Hall had a friend.

"I'm like an amputee," he told Naum. "That woman called, and it was like that phantom limb that's no longer there started hurting."

Icons were the thing that brought them together. Icons and the clairvoyant nineteenth-century Russian healer and spiritual guide Elder Amvrosy, the staretz from Optina Monastery.

Cal loved Elder Amvrosy and the elder's book, *Living Without Hypocrisy*.

Naum kept copies folded in his pocket of the Morning Prayer of the Last Elders of Optina, the prayer that begins: *O Lord, grant that I may meet all that this coming day brings to me with spiritual tranquility. Grant that I may fully surrender myself to Thy holy Will . . .*

When they first met, Naum gave a copy to Pastor Cal.

Cal's office at Holy Communion Protestant Church had no space left on the walls. He'd been to Russia many times. Greece too. Shelf after shelf of patristic works, lives of the saints, liturgical studies, and the many icons Naum thought of as friends who'd gotten lost, friends whom he secretly wanted to take with him under his cassock each time he left Cal's office.

Naum often wanted to ask his friend, "What are you waiting for?" He never had the heart to ask if Cal had read Elder Amvrosy's opinion of Protestantism.

"Our usual breakfast?" Cal said.

The Protestant pastor and the Orthodox priest met early mornings, once a week, at Betty's.

"I hate getting out of bed in the dark," Naum told Cal. "But I'm looking forward to it." Naum made sure they never went to breakfast on a strict fasting day. "Flapjacks cheer me up this time of year."

It was Lenten March, rainy and raw. Naum ducked into the alcove at Betty's and closed his umbrella. Overhead, red neon glowed from the Art Deco cup-and-saucer sign above the entrance. Naum looked at the weather and thought, *Not even a pigeon would be out this early in this weather.*

The 1940s-era coffee shop was crowded for a Monday. Every booth was full. The buzz of conversation above the smell of scrapple, coffee, eggs, and toast made Betty's a cozy place to meet.

The waitress put a cup on the table and asked Naum, "Just you this morning, Padre?"

Naum held up two fingers. "He'll be here." He took off his coat and nestled into the well-worn booth.

Cal came in windy and wet. Rain down his neck made him shiver. It was a long walk from Holy Communion Protestant Church. He turned down his collar and unbuttoned his coat, took his smartphone from his pocket and put it on the table. "Hey, you made it," he said to Naum.

Naum was always happy to see Pastor Cal. He still looked like a military man. Something in his demeanor. There was no hiding his love of order. He used to tell Naum, in German, "*Ordnung muss sein,* Father. Gotta have order."

They ordered the usual. And no meat. The waitress knew they'd be occupying the back booth for quite a while. With regulars in the neighborhood, it was expected. And with the clergy?

But the two friends knew enough to let the tip reflect the fact that their weekly meeting took up table space and tip potential far more than even a leisurely breakfast might allow, the regular and standing subject of the Laney Effect notwithstanding.

Naum listened each time the story was repeated. Each time the telling seemed to soothe things. All his silverware symmetrically arranged, all his napkins neatly folded into origami crosses, Cal would settle down and settle in. He'd stop fiddling with his smartphone. The subject would turn to other, seemingly more manageable things.

Cal said, "You never serve at the ecumenical things."

"I read the epistle," Naum said.

"You see their faces?" Calvin said. "When you finished chanting the epistle?"

Naum didn't answer. Prayer had a source. It wasn't us.

"You realize that's what started me coming to Vespers," Cal said. "That's why I brought my youth group. The Ladies' Society too. You remember when Linda asked you about the Rapture." Cal liked that. He found it amusing.

"Darby, the poor priest," Naum said. "And his disciple Scofield.

Maybe they didn't have much Greek."

"Anglican? At that time? I doubt it. He knew his stuff," Cal said. "They manage the scripture to fit their theology."

"One word, *paralambano*," Naum said.

Cal said, "Yep, one word. But, that's no small thing, Naum. For every single degree you fly off course, one of our Navy pilots told me, you're gonna miss your target by ninety feet or more for every mile you fly."

Naum was listening, eating his butterless flapjacks, but listening. He liked to let others teach him. There was only one Master who did not have to learn what He taught, so the Fathers say.

"That," Cal said, "amounts to about one mile off target for every sixty miles flown. You start at the equator, for instance, and fly around the earth? One little degree off would land you almost five hundred miles off target, and, my friend, the longer you travel off course, the further you end up away from your intended landing. Compass headings are critical, Naum."

Naum, the eternal catechumen, had observed that some people learn best by teaching others. Naum catechized best by allowing himself to be taught.

"Naum, how many sacraments do you guys have?" Pastor Calvin wanted to know.

"You're asking me, how many are the mysterious ways by which God communicates Himself to us. Is that what you're asking?"

"It seems silly when you put it that way."

"How would you put it?" Naum was serious, respectful, and sincere. "Really, Pastor Cal, I'm interested to learn."

"We have two," Cal said. "Baptism and the Eucharist."

"I see."

"There are other things," Cal said. "Confirmation. Penance. Anointing of the sick. Marriage, of course. Not sacraments, though, strictly speaking."

"How about ordination?" Naum asked.

"Holy Orders?" Pastor Cal paused for a minute to sip his coffee. "Well, no. Holy Orders just doesn't go down well with us, the intervention of an ordained priest . . . Not to say it couldn't be a bishop or a pastor, but it's not limited to them either. Could be a government official, an ordinary citizen, a wandering itinerant preacher, maybe even a person who subscribes to a way different from Christianity, who knows?"

"Sounds like a mystery to me." Naum smiled.

"Funny," Cal said.

"So let me understand, then. Why do they need us? Just curious. A little clarity goes a long way when you're trying to understand why your friend's doing what he's doing, believing what he believes.

"You were ordained after years at the seminary. Went through a rigorous review process to be certified, but if ordination isn't a sacrament like the others you mentioned, then can anyone from the congregation, or a government official, an itinerant preacher, even a non-Christian, like you said, can they stand up and give the sermon, conduct the Eucharist, confirm, baptize, or marry?"

Cal wanted to say no, but he said, "Hmm."

Coffee time was coming to an end. The rain was stopping, and daylight was dimming the red neon of Betty's art deco cup and saucer.

Cal looked out the window. Almost to himself, he said, "Real

Presence or just symbolic. I'd like to discuss that some time."

Naum told his friend, "I'd like to be able to explain *unreal* presence."

"That's a thought." Cal said. "Maybe next week?"

———

NAUM WOULD HAVE LIKED TO TELL his friend about symbol as a sign to bring together. "The opposite of *symbol* is not indicated by the word *real*, as in, it's a symbol or it's real. The opposite of *symbol* is *diabole*, to slander, to take a bite, to fragment, to generate confusion and scatter." He wanted to tell his friend, "We both know his name, Cal, Diabolos, *he who takes a bite*."

But instead Naum was quiet. Why take a bite? He said, "Maybe next week. If we remember."

The waitress came and offered refills. Both men declined. It was time to go. Their cups were empty, and this week's talk had reached the brim. Even the clergy have a limit.

Cal had a classical education, some Greek, but mostly Latin. He was half thinking aloud when he said, "*Sacramentum*, the loyalty oath taken by Roman soldiers, the pledge deposited in good faith between disputing parties in a court case."

"I failed Latin," Naum said. "Greek too."

Win the argument, lose the soul, one of Naum's favorite sayings. Under the table, he formed the fingers of his right hand into the sign of the Holy Trinity and asked God for the prayer of the heart. Anyone who can be argued in can be argued out.

"You? Failed Greek?" Cal said, "I believe you're telling me another one of your Kusheri Nastradin stories."

Naum smiled. A good sower knows how and when to prepare

the soil, how and when to scatter the seed, how and when to be still. Naum said, "Did I ever tell you the one called *And the devil went forth to sow his seed?*"

Cal seemed genuinely intrigued. He smiled and slowly said, "No."

"Ask us Orthodox the time, we'll tell you the history of the watch."

"Speaking of which . . ." Cal checked the time on his cell phone and reached for his wallet.

Naum said, "It's my turn."

"I'll leave the tip?"

Naum put the money on the table. He could tell his friend didn't want to go home to the empty parish house.

"Thinking of that call upsets you, Cal, doesn't it?" Naum said. "Laney's call."

Pastor Cal nodded.

Naum asked, "You still talk with the Elder Amvrosy, don't you? When you pray."

"I do," Cal said.

"I understand your daughter Emily called you."

It made Cal smile. The years had been a pitted road.

"You're a good pastor and a good father. You've suffered but haven't turned away from Christ," Naum said.

"By the prayers of the staretz, Christ hasn't turned away from me," said Pastor Lieutenant JG Chaplain Calvin Hall.

"I wish I could remember all the elder's sayings," Naum said.

"Actually, I have one that's been with me a lot lately. Especially when I'm alone. He says something like, when you do good, don't pay any attention if people aren't grateful, and if you expect a reward, you're gonna endure deprivation."

Naum stood to put on his coat. "Walk you to your office, Pastor?"

"Why not? And you're still coming next week, right? To our Visitors' Night, to talk with our people about the icons? It's our biggest turnout, when you come."

"Your ladies are cooking, I'm coming."

"My Emily's gonna be there. You can tell us stories."

Gracious in Adversity

THE BUS PULLED TO THE CURB like a shimmering mirage. A boy said it was Tarzan-hot. Jungle-hot. Her old knees liquefied, barely lifting her up the steps. The driver pinched the rumpled transfer, damp with perspiration, from her hand. There was no seat. News radio said many elderly were dying from the heat. She believed it. Her dress stuck to her, sweaty palms slippery on the vertical galvanized handrail. This was the final leg in a ninety-minute, three-bus relay. Two weeks running. Her husband, Peter, lay comatose in a hospital far across the city.

Fifty years of marriage. Good companions. The house was lonely without him. He drove the car. Took her shopping. Cut the grass. Checked the windows at night. Complained about nothing worth watching on TV and the price of shoes nowadays.

Even his complaining she missed. They loved the Church. Very faithful, those two, about the Church. Both of them always there, doing one thing or another. She missed the Liturgy.

The Teuta Ladies' Baking Society had sent a beautiful flower basket. Very expensive. She'd been part of committees who'd sent them to others. Say it? Never. But she thought it was a waste. A sin almost. So many people needed help. There must be a better way to put that money to use. She could just picture the basket on her dining-room table. After a week the flowers were more than wilted. She scolded herself for not remembering to throw them away. But she had so much to do.

Morning to evening with her Peter. Bathed him. Talked to him. Kept an eye on the feeding tubes and the beeping monitors. Arranged his bedclothes. Turned him over. No bedsores on her boy, not on him. Amarie was determined. Brushed his hair. Kissed his forehead. Staff was amazed at her faithfulness.

She read him morning prayers. Akathists to Our Master and to His Mother. Prayed aloud before the icon of his patron saint that Father Naum had taped on the oxygen apparatus above the bed.

She knew both her Peter and God heard her prayers. She knew it. And she sang to him. And he heard it. Though he couldn't tell her, he loved her company and her voice.

She ate breakfast, lunch, and dinner at the hospital. Fell asleep in the chair next to his bed, held his hand, and dreamt of when they were young.

Eight AM. She struggled from the bus. Her day of service to her husband was just beginning, and already she was exhausted. From behind, she felt cool air on the back of her legs. A taxi door had opened. An elderly woman in a blue sweater got out and said hello. She was carrying flowers to her husband. Same air-conditioned taxi, same time . . . And home again, each evening.

I could never afford a taxi, thought the woman whose name meant *gracious in adversity*. Amarie hobbled through the revolving door, scolding herself once more for forgetting to drop that thank-you card in the mail and for not remembering to throw away those wilted flowers. *Got to be a better way,* she thought, *to put that money to use . . .*

Gather to Me

DOCTOR NICHOLAS, THE SURGEON, came in first and went to his usual place in the church. His beard was white but his hair was still dark, long and dark. He was surprised the front door had been unlocked. Then he heard the women, the Teuta Ladies' Baking Society, upstairs in the hall of Saint Alexander the Whirling Dervish parish. He could smell the Lenten potluck dinner warming in the ovens. He was hungry. Not eating from the noontime hour was something he was used to. Most of Great Lent he lived on very little, according to the prescription he'd arranged with his father confessor. Food aside, it had been a rough day.

He stayed in the back, loosened his tie, and used it to polish his silver-rimmed glasses. He was just hoping to settle down and let the prayer wash over him. He was the kind of tired that made him question whether he'd stopped in the narthex to light a candle and venerate the icons. Boyhood habits. Tired but happy. He knew he probably had. Three candles, one for his wife and kids, one for his patients, and for the third he always said, "God knows the names of those who have no one to pray for them, the ages of each, and their true needs, from their mothers' wombs."

Doctor Nick had not intended to be in the OR that morning. The secretary of the department head had texted him. The department head needed his help. A patient was in trouble. Doctor Nick's younger colleague, now his boss, had made political connections in the hospital hierarchy and had been appointed chief.

It wasn't unusual for Doctor Nicholas to get an emergency call to the OR. Department of Surgery staff had a nickname for Doctor Nick: they called him the Fixer of Last Resort, or just Nick the Fixer.

His young colleague, Department Head Doctor Cathy Kibble, had a nickname too. The perioperative nurses and admin staff called her Killer Kibble. Doctor Nick had saved her, or more exactly, her patients, more often than people would want to know. It was touch and go that morning, he prayed the entire time for the patient and his family, and he was able to save the man on the table, just barely.

The church was empty now. The priest was in the altar doing whatever priests do in the altar prior to Presanctified Liturgy. Doctor Nick the Fixer was happy no one was asking his help. He coveted this time, just to be still.

———•——

MILIA ENTERED THE NARTHEX and lit her candles. Her head-covering helped to hide the tears on her face.

When Danny came home from the putty factory in a bad mood, there was nothing she could do to make him happy. He almost pushed her out the door to Presanctified. The Wednesday evening service and the thought of quiet time to herself, and breaking bread with considerate people at the potluck, made her wish Father Naum would have more weekday Lenten services.

Part of her wished her Danny would come. Another part didn't. She was thankful both girls were away at college now. She'd put up with a lot just to get them where they needed to be. She wasn't sure how much longer she could hang on.

Milia was no pushover, and she wasn't anybody's punching bag. *Threaten all you want, Danny. One time is all it would take for me to be out the door.* She could fend for herself if she had to.

People said she still had her looks. Thank God she was in good health. It'd been a while since she worked outside the home, but she had an education. Milia had never been prone to depression or feeling sorry for herself. She understood everybody was sad from time to time. But she was damned if she was going to shoulder a sadness that only led to more sadness. Milia told Father Naum, "Maybe I can't explain it, but when I have a decision to make, I pray to God, and what happens at Presanctified clears my head like water from a deep old well."

———•———

WHEN IT CAME TO LITURGY, Presanctified or otherwise, Father Basil only wanted to get it over with. The Wednesday evening rush hour traffic up the interstate made him wild.

Matushka Jayne, his wife, sat belted in the passenger seat, her hand clenched tight around the strap above the door, her feet pressed hard on an imaginary brake, and listened to endless rants about redesigning the highway system countrywide.

"Pick a lane," he'd shout. "No matter which lane I get in, that's the one that grinds to a halt." He attended Wednesday evenings only because of her. "Why don't they put a monorail down the middle of these damn highways?"

Jayne was as pleasant and poised as Father was irritable and unhinged. She once thanked Naum, privately, for allowing her husband to serve with him at Saint Alexander's. "None of the other priests want him around," she said.

They were both tall, Jayne and Father Basil, but he was as wide and unwieldy as a forklift. Naum knew he'd suffered in the war. He confessed to Naum. Maybe he'd been put in a positon where he did things a chaplain shouldn't do.

He complained about the length and the selection of the readings and the prayers, about the choir dragging out the hymns. He said to Naum, "Can't ya go any slower, buddy?" Then he'd catch himself. The priest Basil was hurting, wounded in the fabric of his being. Jayne was his only remaining connection to life and to faith.

Sometimes, in the middle of the service, Father Basil would get a starry faraway look. He'd lose his place in the prayers. He'd chatter to Naum, "Who's that guy in the back? He's a doctor, isn't he? Why's he have a beard? Is he married?"

Naum would only say, "Yes, Father."

"Ya got a lot of foreigners here."

"Yes, Father."

"Why's that girl have her head covered? She a nun?"

"Yes, Father." Naum pulled Basil close. "But she's married."

Father Basil would take his cell phone from his cassock, out from under his vestments, and walk through the altar photographing icons, the holy vessels, flowers, and even the charcoal sparking in the censer. He'd go into his hanging vestment bag and take icons he'd painted and place them on the altar table. He'd say to Naum, "Whaddaya think?"

Then when Naum started the censing, and the choir intoned *"Let my prayer arise,"* down on his knees Basil would go, and the big man would weep, sing and weep, enough to break your heart in heaven.

One time he wrote Naum a note.

Yo, Fa-da!

I won't be seeing you this weekend as I am serving in Pleasantville, so I thought I would send this along before it gets mislaid.

Great inspiring sermon at Presanctified. Jayne particularly loved it. She says that mine often get negative—yours never do.

I must tell you that I usually come to your parish with mixed feelings.

Scruffy immigrants are not my cup of tea. To see these guys using cell phones in and out of the building makes me want to give them a cellular colonoscopy.

After that, there is absolutely no place to hang my bag to get out my vestments.

I kind of cover this up with jokes. (Sarcastic jokes)

Then something else happens. I enter into your liturgy and your love for all these folks and I,

1. Feel guilty.

2. Admire you for your wonderful love after all your years.

Then I am moved by the Spirit in the Liturgy and nothing else matters.

You are an island of joy in a sea of cynicism.
What can I say except, thank you.
In my next life I will be Naum.
With deepest brotherly love,
Basil.

After the service, Naum asked Basil, "Father, will you please go up and bless the food? The people are hungry."

Matushka Jayne helped. Milia too. People ate and laughed and forgot, for a while, things in their life that weren't easy to remember.

Madeline, Carol, Ramona, Bernice, and the other members of the Teuta Ladies' Baking Society loved it when Doctor Nick took off his jacket, rolled up his sleeves and his pant legs, put on a pointed paper cap he'd made from a newspaper, got into one of the big trash barrels and jumped up and down, compacting it with his feet.

Two-Beer Eddie, Lefty, and Teddy-the-Horse, Nicky Zeo too, all said, "Now that's my kinda doctor."

Father Basil was shanghaied by the big, gregarious, always happy *foreigner*, Giorgi, and taken to sit with some of the other scruffy immigrant *foreigners* at the table furthest back in the church hall, comparing ringtones, drinking too many tiny cups of *foreign* coffee, and putting each other in smiling happy pixels.

———

LATER THAT SAME LENTEN SEASON, Naum received another note from Father Basil.

Naum, You're a hypocrite. Vindictive. And a coward.

Naum had taken a certain pastoral tack with a hard-to-reach parishioner. He hoped to plant a seed, but it was a hard seed to swallow. People often play one priest against another.

Naum felt bad. "God knows the truth" was all he would say.

He did his best to deflect his brother's praise in the first, complimentary note. He did his best to accept his brother's rebuke in the second note.

Father Naum had known the hard-to-reach parishioner for many years and had tried every tack. The discipline he had applied as a last resort was something he was not at liberty to explain. He hoped in time the bitter pastoral seed would grow into something beneficial for all involved.

A shepherd once explained to Naum, "Far off down the road if I see a tractor-trailer bearing down, most of the sheep will follow me off the easy road onto the rocky shoulder. Some, though, need prodding with the staff for me to gather them safely home."

———

AFTER PRESANCTIFIED, while everyone was upstairs, Naum consumed the Gifts. In a secret place by the table of preparation he kept a verse, Psalm 50:5, embroidered by Olga.

She told him she did it while she was still young, only 75. Thirty full years before she fell asleep in the Lord Jesus.

Taking a moment alone after Holy Communion to stand in front of her embroidery in the darkened altar had become a habit for Naum.

Gather to Me My faithful ones, who made a covenant with Me by sacrifice.

Outside he could hear Giorgi, Doctor Nick, and Father Basil

laughing, carrying bags to the dumpster in the back. Doctor Nick asked Father Basil, "What's he doing in there?"

"The priest?" Basil said. "Whatever priests do in the altar after Presanctified."

Once a Woman

———•———

KOREA WAS WHERE Jimmy's faith lost its life. "Waves of men," he said. He sat with the priest at a memorial meal for his brother Koli.

"Seven kids, my mom had. Koli was the oldest. He married a Spanish girl, got a job as a dance instructor with Arthur Murray Studios, and the son-of-a-gun danced for a living, you believe it? While I went off to Korea.

"The ones in the first row were armed, mighta been with those Type 24 Chiang Kai-Sheks, and coming at us. Christ! Ya couldn't see the end of 'em. The ones in the next row, the row behind the first, didn't have shit—oh, sorry, Father. Sorry. The second rank, all unarmed. Poor suckers. When we cut down the first row, the second row was supposed to pick up their rifles. If they didn't, the guys armed in the third row cut 'em down from behind. We were using M1919 Brownings, air-cooled, side-fed. Even pouring water on them we couldn't . . ."

Naum didn't move.

"It was like wave after wave, worse than the slaughterhouse used ta be here in the neighborhood, 'member, when we were kids? You know I was an altar boy, Father, but after that? I mean, I was still only a kid myself, nineteen. You don't know what a thirty-caliber round'll do to the human body. I'm sorry, Father, but you ask yourself, where in the hell is God? Whaddaya supposed ta do after that? Came back here and went to barber school like Lefty, on the GI Bill."

It was Jimmy's wife, Diane, who got him back to church. She'd been raised Catholic, gone to Catholic schools, loved the Virgin, and there was even a time when red-headed Diane thought about becoming a nun. Then she met Jimmy boy.

She signed papers. He signed them too, when they were married, promising to raise the kids Catholic. They were married in her church, Saint Boniface Cathedral.

Father Naum asked if once a month, even six times a year, they could come to Liturgy. "If you like," he said, "come to confession, Jimmy. We can find a way to bless the marriage here, if you and Diane like."

Naum never knew why, but Diane started showing up at Liturgy with the kids. At first she stayed in the back and left before coffee hour. Then she started sitting with Jimmy's sister Margie. Margie was the sweet sister.

The crazy sister, Eleanor, used to stand in the middle of Liturgy and call out, "Now, Father, that's not how it was done in my mother's day. You have to ring the bells so we know when to stand or sit, and ring them for Communion too."

Eleanor was full of rules, rules for fasting, rules for how to dress, how many times to bow: "All the way down, forehead on the floor." She'd look at the kids and tell Diane, "A good ear-pull'll straighten 'em out, but ya gotta do it when they're young."

Eleanor was pretty glad-handed with Diane's kids, little Jim and Emily, a little too glad-handed for Diane's taste.

Diane told Margie, the sweet sister, "I had a nun like Eleanor in third grade. Mister Sister, we called her."

The kids grew and went away to college. Church was not on the syllabus. Jimmy followed Diane back to Saint Alexander the Whirling Dervish Orthodox Church.

He'd pick up the books she left around the house. He never knew there were so many books in English about the Orthodox Church.

On the Incarnation, by Saint Athanasios, was his favorite, one of the ones that made sense, jived up with what he'd seen and experienced.

> *This, then, was the plight of men . . .*
>
> *God created man for incorruption and as an image of His own eternity; but by envy of the devil death entered into the world . . .*
>
> *When this happened, men began to die . . .*
>
> *Adulteries and thefts were everywhere, murder and raping filled the earth, law was disregarded in corruption and injustice, all kinds of iniquities were perpetrated by all, both singly and in common . . .*
>
> *Cities were warring with cities, nations were rising against nations, and the whole earth was rent with factions and battles, while each strove to outdo the other in wickedness.*

Whoever this Athanasios guy was, he made more than a lot of sense to Jimmy.

When Diane was chrismated, she made Jimmy promise he'd

come once in a while. "Even just to protect me from your sister Eleanor."

He told her he was only coming 'cause an old army buddy called Athanasios had talked him into taking a second look.

She said, "Why don't you invite him to dinner?"

Jimmy said, "Just deployed, him and his family, overseas. Maybe when they get back."

Diane became active in every aspect of parish life. She loved the Church. Kept the fasts. Learned to make the holy bread. Never missed Vespers or Liturgy, and her confessions were always aimed at herself, for her growth in *life, faith, and spiritual understanding.*

It was the time Diane made him come to confession that started Jimmy realizing that

> *. . . the genesis of the world is the beginning of time, and this beginning is not yet time, not even a fraction of time, just as the beginning of a road is not yet the road itself, that a house you were just starting to build wasn't the house.*

. . . that one part of him was not the whole of him.

When he read those words by Saint Basil the Great, Jimmy figured knowing God was the same too.

Naum and Jimmy the barber became fixtures at the Double Eagle Coffee Shop. They met the same day, same time, same table, every week. No subject was off limits. Jimmy wasn't always the one with the questions. And Naum wasn't always the one with the answers. They were just friends.

WHEN THE ALZHEIMER'S SET IN, Diane changed. When she peed on the floor by the candle stand in the narthex in front of the icon of Saint Matrona the Blind, Jimmy told Naum, "Once a woman, twice a child."

Jimmy was out in the sun trimming hedges when Naum visited them at home. He got happy when he saw the priest. "Hey, Padre! C'mon in, bring your coffee, take off your hat. Take a break on the porch."

Diane was wandering the yard collecting dandelions and weeds into scraggly bouquets. While Jimmy and Naum talked on the porch, Diane came from behind and took Naum's priest hat, the skufia, and the paper cup full of coffee he brought with him.

When Naum looked again she'd turned the cup and his hat into well-watered potted plants, soil and all. Jimmy didn't cry when she smiled and offered Naum her bouquet of dandelion weeds.

Naum thanked her.

She said "Welcome."

Then it got to be Mass, Mass at least twice a week, back at Saint Bonnie's. She would dress like a schoolgirl, ankle socks and penny loafers, the long skirt and hat, with the white blouse and her old school sweater, and Jimmy would take her.

Diane was his girl. She would always be his girl. Something about hearing the Mass, her fingers entwined in her rosary, and Jimmy there holding her hand, just the way he smelled when she leaned on his shoulder and he took and kissed her hand, something about all that seemed to calm Diane, and Jimmy too.

When Diane's sister died, the funeral Mass was in Saint Boniface Cathedral. It was a Monday. Naum was invited. He was the man in the cassock, back by the holy water cistern. He took off his skufia and stood near the statue of the Virgin.

The family sat in the front pews, and at Communion time, Jimmy stood in line with Diane, holding her hand. Jimmy was communed, and then Diane too.

Eleanor the irascible turned in the pew to give Naum a glare that made him wish he wasn't there.

For two Sundays in a row, no Jimmy. No Diane. Then on the third Sunday, early, before Orthros, the deacon told Father Naum, "There's a man and a woman here asking for a minute of your time."

Naum was vested, except for the *phelonion*. He exited the deacon's door. When he saw Jimmy and Diane huddled close in the front pew, he was happy and sad at the same time.

"Father," Jimmy said. Diane sat there in her schoolgirl outfit, smiling. Naum wasn't sure what she was seeing, but she was smiling at the icon of the Theotokos as if she were hearing the Holy Mother speaking to her.

"Mass is the only thing that lets her sleep," Jimmy said. "If I don't go to Communion with her, she won't go, and then it's hell all week. She's afraid to go anywhere without me. I know we've excommunicated ourselves, Father, but God is all we have." Tears were running down his face. He sat with her hand in both of his.

In Korea, a nineteen-year-old boy facing a human wave, behind a thirty-caliber M1919 Browning air-cooled machine gun, lost his faith and wanted to know.

Naum knew. He wanted to know too.

When he called the bishop's office, Naum tried to remember Saint Basil, about the beginning of the road as not yet the road itself, and the beginning of time being not yet time, not even a fraction of time. But before he could conclude his appeal, the bishop said to him, "You've been ordained now longer than I, Father. God bless them, and you."

One Button

—•—

"I have a question, Father, regarding my sons." Samuel Elias was very old. His sons were no longer children. Samuel had hair, lots of it, combed straight back, white, six inches down over the collar of his collar-buttoned white shirt and lopsided dark blue sweater. One button was missing from his favorite thread-end cardigan, and two buttons were buttoned in the wrong holes. Samuel Elias wore a tie, but only on Sundays.

His wife Magdalena tch-tched about his long beard. She said, "It makes you look like Ben Gunn."

"I like Ben Gunn," Samuel said.

"If only pirates would maroon you," she told him.

"I would thrive on Treasure Island."

"Treasure Island, my fanny."

Mister Elias had been an old man when Father Naum was a boy. Naum remembered him, even then, walking with a *bastun*, a wooden cane that had belonged to Samuel's father, also called Samuel. Samuel the First.

And Naum remembered the current Samuel's wife too, from his boyhood in the church. Magdalena, the woman with the beautiful eyes who taught church school, refused to sing in the choir because she claimed the choir director at the time, Lisa Tazo, wore men's underwear. Where Magdalena got that notion? Better not to ask.

Magdalena Elias wore long dresses, her head was always covered, but gold earrings? She couldn't resist. Magdalena baked prosphora so good, the boys serving in the altar couldn't wait till after Holy Communion. They hid the large portion of her bread the priest hadn't used when he prepared the Holy Communion in the pre-Liturgy service called *proskomedia*, and after Liturgy, they gobbled all of Magdalena's meshe, ate it all for themselves.

"Now if you interrupt me," Samuel told Naum, "I won't be able to finish." They sat together drinking tea on the sunny enclosed front porch of the Elias house. Magdalena was in the kitchen baking *byrek*, the spinach-feta filo pie others call *spanakopita*.

The Fathers say you can listen another's soul back into existence. The more Naum heard, the less he liked to talk, and the less he talked, the more he liked not being heard.

"I had a rocking chair," Samuel Elias began, "from 1919. Yes, my father bought it used off the junk man who used to come through the neighborhood the day after trash day with his horse and wagon. On trash day, he'd collect stuff off the curb, fix it up, and turn around and sell it. Can you believe? Well, my father cleaned it up, this rocker he bought from the junkman, put it in the bedroom, and my pregnant mother, God give her peace, rocked me in it even before I was born."

Naum knew that old wooden rocking chair. He'd seen it. Anyone could see how beautifully worn, powder-smooth and almost white, the seat, the arms, the rockers and rails were. At the beginning of each year, it was the custom for the priest to visit every home with the water blessed at the Feast of Theophany, going through each room using a bouquet of fresh basil, sprinkling the blessed water, chanting and asking God's blessing on the family and the household. And on that bedroom rocking chair.

When Thou, O Lord, wast baptized in the Jordan,
The worship of the Trinity was made manifest.
For the voice of the Father bore witness to Thee,
And called Thee His beloved Son.
And the Spirit, like in the form of a dove,
Confirmed the truthfulness of His word.

"So my older son, Haralambos, you know, Father, we always called him Harry, he wanted that chair in the worst way. He'd been rocked in it himself. His brother, Petrach, too. We called him Petey. I loved those little boys. Slept in the same bed. Played all day together. You remember them, altar boys, both of them. Harry with the blond hair, straight as string. Pete, wavy, wavy isn't the word, thick and wavy and dark. I can smell them. Kiss them on the head and smell them. I would've fought heaven and hell for my boys. Sorry, Father."

Harry was the college professor. Harry was the deacon. Harry was the religious one. Naum had been to their house. Harry and his wife, Christine. Christine the PhD. Christine the educator. Head covered in church, with a skirt to the ground, but on the job at the university, the epitome of strict gray form following no-nonsense function, severe and austere as academic sin in administrative attire.

When Naum visited the home, Christine greeted him at the front and directed him around to the side entrance of what she and Deacon Haralambos called their mini-mansion. "Only people we don't know come to the front," she said. "You just missed my father-in-law. He helped Harry move the new oriental carpet we have in the den."

"She never even invites me in," Samuel said. "I go to the door, she peeks out, opens it a crack, I'm standing there like a supplicant. 'I have your mail,' I say. 'I've been collecting like you asked when you were away.' I smell something cooking. I say, 'Something smells good.' She says, 'I'm cooking.' Takes the mail, says, 'Thank you. I'll tell Harry you were here.' And there I am, looking at the big mahogany front door with the sidelights and the transom, and the brass fittings burnished just right, with the circular brass doorknob in the middle of the front door staring me in the face like the cyclops daring Odysseus, me, their father, the beggar on the doorstep of the manor house."

Samuel Elias seemed very sad to Naum. Sad beyond sad. The kind of sad where you keep taking deep breaths and still never get enough air to do more than sigh.

"You know, Naum," he said, "someone who works at the school where he teaches, tells *me*, tells me, *my* Harry?" Samuel said it like a question. "Harry tells people his professor, his mentor, my son tells people at the school, this man, his mentor, is his true father. *My Harry* says this?"

Naum knew Deacon Harry. He knew Petrach too. Petrach with the long hair. Petrach with the tattoos. Petrach the guitar player. Owner of the type of dog people crossed the street to avoid, the type of dog his parents would not allow at their house.

The son who was always short of money. "He uses foul language, my Petey," Samuel said, "in front of his mother. If I'd done such a thing? I wouldn't even think of it, not even after coming home from the war."

Samuel Elias paused for a moment. He said, "And he blames me. He said, 'This happened on your watch.' I put my head down and pointed up in my heart and said the same thing to Him."

A rare parent, Naum knew, who died with unbroken heart.

"Father Naum," old Samuel said, "I went to see Harry three times during Great Lent. I fasted. I prayed. I gave to the poor. I did things, yard work and shopping, for my neighbor, she's a shut-in. I read the Fathers. Magdalena and I read the Scripture appointed by the Church and we prayed together every night before bed. I got up in the middle of the night and prayed for everyone I could think of, living and dead, and asked them to pray for my family and for me.

"The first visit," Samuel said, "Harry was alone at his house. 'Think carefully,' I told him. 'It could be, one or more of your cousins was abused as a child by one of the uncles.' You know, Naum," Samuel Elias said, "Magdalena is from a very large family. Harry just looked at me. 'Are you sure?' he said. 'What are you up to, Detective Dimitri?' That's what they used to call me when they were boys and they knew I was on the hunt for something.

"I said, 'Think it over, Harry. Have you heard anything? Do you remember anything that might be an indication? Nothing ever happened to you, did it, Harry?' He put me at ease. 'No, Pop.' He said, 'Don't be silly.' It did my heart good to have my son comfort me."

Family is probably the only place where emotions run as deep as they do in a parish community. Naum heard an older priest say blood is thicker than water, and chrism is thicker than blood. And when the two run together, oh bo-bo.

"I went back a second time," Samuel said. "I told Harry I would be coming back. 'Have you thought of anything, son?' He told me, no. 'Okay. I'm on the trail,' I said. 'I just want to be sure you're okay.' He told me he was fine. He said, 'Why are you asking now? Is there something I should know about?' Maybe he was worried, but with Harry, it isn't always easy to tell. When he's worried, he's nonchalant. When he seems unconcerned, who knows? He may be worried."

Samuel continued, "'Let me put it this way,' I said to Harry. 'What if one of the uncles had taken the kids into the garage and gave them drink or got them to smoke marijuana and showed them pornographic material, and then . . .'

"He looked at me like I was crazy, Naum. What could I do? I shrugged and said, 'Well, okay then, Harry.' We talked about his job at the university. He told me about his duties as a deacon. He's particularly involved with the young people at his parish."

Father Naum knew the parish. He knew Deacon Harry's reputation for being zealous about the canons. Students often said he was a *letter of the law* kind of guy. But they liked him just the same. Student reviews on the university's rate-your-professor website featured Harry as a good listener, empathetic, hard but fair, someone who had a way of putting people at ease.

"The third time," Samuel Elias said, "I asked Harry to meet me at the coffee shop downtown. You know the one. I had the rocking chair in the backseat of my car. Let me tell you, Naum, it wasn't easy getting it in there. And on the seat next to me I had a copy of the canons. 'Can I have it?' Harry would always ask about the canons. 'Just to borrow,' he would say. 'Harry,' I told him, 'I'll buy you one. Goodness, it only cost me nineteen dollars on sale.' He laughed. 'Pop, look on Amazon. *If* you can find one nowadays, fifteen hundred minimum.' I was shocked, Naum.

"That aside, 'Harry,' I said, 'I'm almost finished looking into what I'm looking into, you know, about the uncle and the cousins. You don't know how much I hate to ask you again, but, once more, anything?' He said, 'No.' 'You're sure?' I said. 'You never heard of anything or saw anything that might make you wonder?' He again told me, 'No.' 'And no one ever touched you,' I asked my son, 'or tried to get you to drink or do drugs, or showed you stuff, or talked to you in a lewd way, or did anything inappropriate to you?' And I hated this to even come out of my mouth, 'Not a school nurse, or a teacher, or a priest . . . or your mother . . . or me?' 'No, Pop,' he said. And it seemed to me the amalgam of a strange emotional mask was forming on his face.

"So there we were at the coffee shop, in public. I wanted to be in a public place. I told him. 'Your brother, Petrach? He left his wife.' I could tell Harry was surprised, but not too surprised. 'His wife tells me she gave him a choice, her or smoking marijuana. Petrach packed up and left. He was staying out all hours. You know his job in the homeless shelter is stressful, and he doesn't make a lot of money. I guess it all became too much when he brought home bedbugs and had to put all of their clothes and furniture on the curb. He had a meltdown at work. They tried to calm him down, but he went wild. He walked out. Harry, the Professor Deacon said, 'Petey quit his job?' 'He quit,' I said. 'And Harry, your brother Petrach told me there is no God. I haven't told your mother any of this. I wanted to talk with you first. He will not come to church. He tells me God is my imaginary friend and my faith is a symptom of my mental illness."

If a well-meaning friend had pulled the thread hanging from Samuel's blue button-down crooked cardigan, with the one button missing and two buttons in the wrong holes, no doubt it would have completely unraveled. Naum knew to remain quiet. Why unravel his old friend's heart?

Samuel Elias, who, Naum knew, always called God his portion in the land of the living. Samuel said to Naum, "And I told Harry, my firstborn, 'Harry, he blames it all on you. Petey says you molested him over a period of years. He went into detail, Harry. Details a father shouldn't have to hear, things no one should do to a child.' Father Naum," the old man said, "I couldn't bring myself to say anything more to Harry."

Harry the upright. Harry the married. Prosperous, personable, Harry the professor deacon with the luminous vestments and the glowing college website reviews.

"I have a question," Samuel Elias had said when Naum first came into the house and sat down.

Petrach the servant of the homeless. Petrach the musician and the artist. Wild Petrach. Tattooed Petrach. Always on the edge. Wounded, wounded in his soul, Petey Petrach.

What question could this father conceive? What answer did the old man hope to offer to the woman who had given birth to these boys all those years ago? Comfort? Vengeance? A miracle? Naum wondered. What was Samuel Elias seeking? Was he asking, where was God?

Old Mister Elias was reduced to a whisper. "You know what

Harry said? Harry, my Harry said to me, 'I guess this is going to ruin my career.' I didn't need anything further, Naum. You're a father. You know your children. I said, 'Harry, walk me to the car.' We left our coffee untouched on the wobbly café table. I had him take the rocker and the canons from the car. I kissed him, Naum. I told my boy, 'I'm not telling your mother, or your wife. I'm not telling your employer or your bishop. None of our relatives. God knows what you do from here. Don't see me or your mother again, Harry, boy that I love, never again, this side of the *Parousia*.' I watched him walk away carrying the rocker and the canons. My son said nothing. He did not look back."

Naum was sunken like a mud-filled room after the waters of a hurricane subside. Old Elias was right there with him. Both trapped in the mud, pinned by the debris, unable to move or speak. The Parousia, the Second Coming. What if he repents and goes to his brother and asks forgiveness and confesses his sin? No, thought Naum. I may not ask. I may not interrupt. I may not comment. I may not criticize, or trivialize with the offer of solutions, scriptural quotes, or spiritual recommendations. *Do not quench the Spirit.* Listening may lead to life.

"Now all my attention, my resources, my money and time are for my Pete," the old man said. "He's angry. He yells at me, 'It happened on your watch.' Father Naum, I never ask him, 'Why didn't you tell us, Mother and me?' I don't ask. I don't defend myself. What's to defend? I allow the hurt of his anger to wither me so nothing remains of any ego that may come between me and my beloved boy. I examine the situation and myself, again and again. Why didn't I see it? We always told them, 'If anyone, *anyone*, school nurse, teacher, priest, even one of us touches you or does anything to make you feel weird, you know when it's wrong, aunts, uncles, anyone, please, tell us.' But what's the good in all that now? What would I have done had he told me, maybe take Harry to the river in a sack like my father used to do with unwanted pups? And I wonder, Harry must be hurting. He has to be. Has Harry gone to confession? Has he told his wife? Has he sought help? Has he begged his brother? Has he tried to make amends? How does he serve at the altar?

"And my Petrach?" Samuel was weeping now. "Will God leave him like this, is there no way back? Will God leave *us*, our family, broken apart like this? Words, or Bible quotes, or ceremonies, nothing, the counseling, the therapy we're spending our retirement on, and believe me, we'd do it ten times over for our boy, but the extent of this infection is like veins of mold that spread in old bread and go beyond anything this side of the grave."

Every word made Naum think of his own failings as a father and as a priest. But this wasn't about him. *Set a watch, O Lord, before my mouth, and keep the doors of my lips.* He tried to be as still as he could. He prayed for stillness, both within and in his outward demeanor.

Naum knew what the old man had said was true. From the time of our expulsion from the paradise of bliss, there was no life without suffering.

And it came to pass, when they were in the field, that Cain rose up against Abel his brother, and slew him.

Cain suffered his punishment in the prison of his ego. He took his brother's life, rent the fabric of his own being, and wandered lost in endless searching.

Finally Samuel Elias asked, "So here is my question. Which

one, Father, or will neither of my sons go to heaven?"

Naum looked toward the kitchen. Samuel sighed. They could hear Magdalena singing the hymn of Kassiani the Nun.

O my Savior, Deliverer of my soul, turn not away from Thy hand-maiden, O Thou of boundless mercy.

Naum didn't ask why she was singing. She must know. Magdalena more than knew. They were one soul in two bodies, Magdalena and Samuel.

Samuel said, "And knowing what I know, will I?"

Naum leaned forward across the space. He unbuttoned the old man's sweater, adjusting each button to its proper hole. He tugged at the corners to align the sweater, and sat back in the icon of silence Samuel had written with his words, and inwardly prayed to resist the temptation of pulling at the one loose thread.

When the time had passed, Naum laid his hands on Samuel's knees. They put their foreheads together.

Naum said, "Mister Elias, Uncle Sammy, you remember when I was newly ordained and you used to come in the altar before Liturgy and un-crooked my vestments and give me kind advice about this particular situation, or that one particular person who loved trouble, or some poor lost soul, writing their names on scraps of paper so I would remember to pray for them, and helping me to know which one was which? You were like an angel. You were a good father to me."

Samuel Elias remembered.

Late morning sun curled the peeling paint on the old porch and warmed the enclosed space through panes of wavy old glass.

Magdalena called from her kitchen. The lamentation in her voice gave away what her words would never say. "Come, Ben

Gunn, bring your beard, and your broken heart, and the priest, too. Can't you smell the byrek?"

Their foreheads still touching, Elias said, "And you know, Father, the sad thing is, it takes only one missing button for the whole vestment to be undone."

Scum. Crime. Filth. Slime.

———

After the Divine Liturgy
The ark retains a certain eucharistic peacefulness
When the Church has been gathered up
Into the bridal chamber of her Master.
Each candle lingers in its own halo of prayer
And gives the narthex light a temple hue.
Overhead a great cloud of witnesses
Rises to the homeland of our hearts' desire
And echoes like an antiphonal choir
In that longed-for day without evening.
But not everyone is touched to the same depth.
Two women stood in the back after Liturgy.
Eris berated Althea.
"Scum. Crime. Filth. Slime."
Imagine, almost like a Dr. Seuss rhyme.

THIS SCOLDING CAUSED such a disturbance in the noetic angels ascending on the incense that even the priest coming from divesting, from consuming the Gifts, tying up his cassock,

eating antidoron, descending down through the deacon's door—
even the priest could tell something wasn't right.

Althea was bent in shame in front of Eris. Further bent than a
supplicant under the confessional stole.

Father Naum approached the two women, hoping for the best.
For over a decade he had appealed to the people of Saint Alexander the Whirling Dervish Orthodox Church, saying, "You are
icons of a different Kingdom."

Again and again he would say, "When will we recognize that
we are the church of the broken toys, that we share each other's
sins, are on the same road, share—at one time or another—similar burdens? All lost children of the one God—strangers in a
strange land, bound together on the same mystifying pilgrimage,
facing the same mystifying end. Then we see that we must stop
breaking each other. We must help each other, praying God will
grant us strength to change from being all about 'me' . . . We
must change in the way we relate to Him, to His creation, and to
all others, to love one another even as He has loved us, especially
when things go wrong."

But no, more coals—Eris was furious. She chastised Althea
even more and then turned on the priest. "Don't talk to me about
love and forgiveness. Get with reality! You have let a criminal in
this church. Her husband lied to me. He chose to commandeer
my money, and she chose to disregard the obvious. He told me he
was sick and bilked me out of money. Now when I ask her, she
tells me he's a drug addict and tries to pay me back this pittance,
this measly partial payment."

Naum was sad.

But Eris couldn't stop herself. "You should stand up in front of the congregation and tell them there is a snake in their midst, her and her whole family. Then maybe you would be doing us a service. You help this, this"—a look toward Althea, derisive as a slap—"and give people like me neither the consideration nor the simple courtesy of a warning."

Father Naum said, "Eris, how much have we been forgiven by Christ?"

But she wouldn't hear it.

Then he said, "Who knows? Maybe one day, you and I, maybe we'll have a problem in our family. And someone will help us instead of announcing it abroad."

"Never," Eris said. "My family is not criminal. We are not low-life scum. I despise her and her ilk—and her rabble kids." She turned to leave, saying, "I will be submitting a delineated request for payment to the parish treasurer. I will see you in court if necessary, both of you!"

Eris was a pragmatist, wise in the way of devils. Nobody's fool. Steeped in the ways of men and children of this world.

Just then, Nicky Zeo, who was parish treasurer that year, came by. Naum asked Eris, "Wait. How much?"

Eris told him the full amount she was owed.

Nicky said, "We have that in the poor fund."

And Eris was paid.

—·—

FATHER NAUM REALIZED THAT FOR NOW, the money was all Eris was capable of receiving. And he knew she needed it and deserved to be repaid. But not like this. How could this be good for anyone?

He wished Eris had come to him first before giving money. It's not always the loving thing to do. Not everyone knows everything, not even the priest—maybe especially the priest.

Althea. Althea the doubly wounded said nothing.

Naum knew she'd been trying to keep her family together in the face of her husband's problems. Two jobs, caring for the kids, keeping up with the rent, trips to doctors and rehabs. Having to humble herself, a professional woman, and beg for help. Brokenhearted by the man she still loved. And every week, she and her "rabble" kids were at church. She read the epistle in her language for the people. She sang in the choir.

Her husband had come to church only to trick Eris. And he did.

He fooled the bread-eating priest too. Yes, Naum had given money.

But Althea, his wife, he did not fool.

The choir came for practice. Althea went with them to the *kliros*.

As they were singing, Naum found deep in the pocket of his cassock a crunchy piece of last week's bread. It was dry. It had a nutty flavor, like *The Way of the Pilgrim*. It made him say the prayer of the heart. For some reason he liked what our people called nafora, the antidoron—he liked it dried.

He would call Eris later in the week. For now, she thinks she's been made whole. Some things and people are better left to season for a while.

Choir voices accompanied Naum as far as the coffee-hour border, where the incense met the sugared fragrance of the coffee and doughnuts, Ramona's kurabia cookies, and the love-made-edible offerings of the Teuta Ladies' Baking Society.

No looking back, Naum. Enter singing. Tripping on your cassock, carried away into that far and distant land.

Praise the Dead

———•———

asn't he left yet?" The calls kept coming.

"Where is that goddamn, good-for-nothing priest?"

"Please, sir, he's on his way," Priftereshe said.

"Why isn't he here yet?"

Priftereshe Greta, the wife of the priest, tried her best, but the calls continued until her husband arrived at the house where he'd been previously uninvited.

All the lights were on. All the doors and windows were open. The house was a flat, one-story rectangle of red-brown brick. The brown shingle roof with the appearance of resawn shake was unusual for a low-profile house of brick.

The front door and the shutters were brown with brass fittings. Forest green trim outlined the geometric shapes on all the doors, windows, eaves, and overhangs. All the custom architectural features were vividly outlined like a child's Crayola drawing of a house.

Vasil Vasili's house might have been a lodge. A fine brick path wound through tall pitch pines, solid white oaks, and gray birch with twisted, papery bark trunks. The hedges were high and well trimmed. The lawn was too green for autumn. There were cars parked like abandoned children's toys all over Vasil Vasili's fine lawn and all over the lawns of his neighbors, right and left.

The black and silver hearse was neatly angled, its curtained back door hanging open on its hinges, positioned precisely at the gaping kitchen door.

The heart of the newly ordained priest pounded. He asked himself, "Why am I here?" He whispered to himself as he stared at his feet, following the rolling brick walk. "'Yea, though I walk through the valley of the shadow of death, I will fear no evil, for Thou art with me.'"

As he was putting on his skufia, a shrieking in-law, the one who'd made all the calls, jerked him by the arm, not giving him time to answer, "Where the *hell* have you been?"

Later he found he had been less than four minutes in arriving. He liked to think he would not have defended himself or made excuses either way. But that night in bed, he played it over again and again, staring at the ceiling in the dark.

Then, the husband, the man who hated priests, his neck blue and bloated out of the collar of his tartan green flannel shirt. Vasil Vasili, feet swollen in clean white socks, like scallion-bulbs out the bottom of his favorite root-beer corduroys. Vasil Vasili, sprawling on his side, stiff with rigor mortis on the indoor-outdoor carpet of the ashen kitchen floor.

He'd been home alone. No one knew how long. Even with all the doors and windows open, every house cavity and recess was steeped in the olfactory wake of his departure. In the eastern corner of the kitchen on a shelf overlooking the body, a red electric candle illumined an icon of Saint Basil.

With quiet decorum the undertaker's men, their cigarettes stubbed out, stood in the familiar posture of rehearsed respect and waited as Father Naum nervously lit the censer and the candles, placed the epitrahilion—the purple one—about his neck, opened the prayer book, and began.

Prayers at the Parting of the Soul from the Body
. . . having accepted the image, but preserved it not, and because, also, that evil be not eternal, Thou hast ordained, through Thy love for mankind, dissolution of the same; and as God of our Fathers, through Thy Divine Will . . . Thou hast cleft and dissolved this insoluble bond, that the body should be dissolved into the elements of which it was fashioned . . .

After the prayers were completed, the fact that the family had stood with him, and so many voices had joined in the Lord's Prayer with him in both languages, English and their native tongue—this surprised the priest and calmed him so that he stopped grinding his teeth.

Vasil Vasili was a heavy man. Naum helped them zip the bulky plastic bag and lift him to a stretcher that elevated like a scissor lift. It had wheels. Vasil Vasili, they took away.

———

MANY TIMES DURING HIS YEARS at the seminary, the seminary housed on the grounds of the monastery, many times Naum helped in the cemetery. Dig here. At a certain depth, the soil changed color. Bones. Bits. Buttons from vestments. A holy water bottle with the cap rotted off with soil now filling the vessel.

And one time, the seminarians had to put their shovels aside
. . . The hair and beard, perfect. The vestments and the Book,
undisturbed. The complexion as if breath still refreshed it, hands,
face, fingers, forehead, lips, incorrupt. It was more than the
young seminarian wished to have explained. The old monks had
engendered in the students a love of stories. Parables were what
our Master used, they said. Experience over explanation.

IN A BRIGHTLY LIT ROOM that smelled of camphor-flakes, the
widow sat, eyes closed, on a plastic-covered mustard yellow sofa.
She was surrounded on both sides, huddled by sisters and sons—
many people unknown to Naum, standing and sitting in the too-
bright room with the oversized lamps and Italianate décor. They
seemed to be waiting for something to happen. The television
was playing, but no one was paying attention.

The widow alone stood when the priest entered the room.
He'd seen her before in church. Regal, is how he would have
described her bearing. Tall, always gracious. If the parish had a
royal daughter, he thought, it would be Jenny. Her hair was pure
white. Once a week, she told him, she had it done. Simple jewelry. Muted fabric and colors in clothing, shoes, and handbags.
Never showy or overdone. Jenny was the classic lady, everything
about her. Friendly, but not overly so. Always willing to listen
and lend a hand, and the kind of woman who left one guessing
about her age. Vasil Vasili was the only accessory that didn't seem
to match. But there, that was love, wasn't it?

Now, for the first time, Naum noticed Jenny looked very tired,
very old. Why hadn't he noticed before? She kissed his hand. He

put his arms around her and held her tightly to stop the shivering, but the room and all that was in it seemed to have been drained of life's very warmth, and he felt as if the blood had stopped flowing, even in his own veins.

Jenny felt unexpectantly pliant, like a little child, sobbing, but only dry tears now. "He's gone. He's gone, oh, Father. I hate him. I hate him."

According to the ancient custom of our people, standing on the porch by the door of the parish house when the priest returned home was a pitcher of water. Priftereshe made sure it was there.

Vasil Vasili. Never a kind word for any priest. *The way he reads the Gospel. The book he uses. The part in his hair. Vestments too short. Vestments too long. Beard. No beard. Too much in our business. Never around. Sermons so boring. Sermons too long. Too eloquent. Too tall. Too short. So fat. Sweats too much. Overeats. Lacking erudition.*

The young priest knew the petitions of Vasil's unhappy priest-litany by heart.

Too damn emotional. No common touch. Overdoes with the big words. Not enough time with the children. Why's he always around the boys. Not spending enough time with the shut-ins. Looking too long at the girls. Money. Money. Money. Talks about it too much. Doesn't push for it enough. Hide your wife. Count the silverware. The man never takes a drink. You think he would dance one time. The last priest let his wife dance with us men. Drinks like a sailor. Curses like one too. Always in the parish house. Misses hospital visits again and again. Never at home. Can't find him when you need him. Invisible six days a week and incomprehensible on the seventh.

If my son . . . Now there would've been a priest. But why waste all that education? Like my grandfather, the oikonomos, *an elevated*

archpriest who knew a thing or two about how to manage a franchise.
I myself would have been a priest, were it not for Jenny—had to go
and marry someone outside the clan.

Naum never knew. Until after the funeral, sitting and talking
with the family. He truly never knew. She'd been in the Communion line with all the ladies of the Teuta Ladies' Baking Society from the first time he'd served. No one ever said a thing.
Jenny spoke the dialect language of the homeland better than
the priest. She knew, no, was famous for her ethnic cuisine. She
crossed herself the way we do. She wore a Byzantine baptismal
cross. She kept the fasts. Jenny sang in the choir. Baptized her
grandchildren. Sewed the altar covers and servers' robes. Baked
the most perfectly formed meshes every week. Never, never
missed a Lenten or Holy Week service. Put up with Vasil Vasili.
Got married in his church, even though her parents disowned
her till the babies came.

"Chrismation," Naum suggested to her, to unite them even
further, beyond death. He leaned in to ask her, "Jenny, what do
you think?" The widow's chair stood empty, along with the one
next to her at the head table at the memorial meal, the chair
always reserved for the priest.

"I've been waiting, Father Naum, for years," she said. "Thank
you for finally asking." Then she said, "You know you were his
favorite."

"Really?" Well, this was a surprise.

"Yes, of all of them. I wanted you to know. And my family
thinks you're wonderful too. You were very patient with us, and I
wanted to thank you. I know my son and my son-in-law behaved
badly. He's excitable, my son, like his father. Can you imagine

Vasil wanted him to be a priest? I am grateful. How you maintained your composure with us, I'm sure I don't know. And they were saying it's so nice to have a young priest for a change, one who speaks English. You have a beautiful singing voice. My sisters think you're just charming. And please, apologize to your wife."

People were coming to the table, shaking his hand and repeating all the things Jenny had told him. Men gave him hugs and tried to slip him folded bills. Ladies kissed him on the cheek. Aftershave and perfume infused his cassock. He had lipstick in his beard. Jenny handed him an envelope from her bag. He knew there was money in it.

"We want you to have this, for you, not the church. Saint Alexander has enough money, and they don't use it for anything. It's like giving money to a bank. Take your wife to dinner. You've been very good to us and found a way to say such kind things about Vasil. Yes, you were his favorite. Out of all of them. He said so many times."

"Thank you," said Naum, reluctant to feel one way or the other. He'd only told the truth about Vasil Vasili, the grandson of a priest who, with all he seemed to know, could have done so much more to be an icon of Christ, but people hear what they hear.

"Half the time, you weren't so bad. He'd say that many a Sunday on the way home," Jenny told Naum.

It confused Naum for a moment, and then he said, "Vasil said that?" It made the priest smile. Praise from the dead.

"Yes," said Jenny. "And coming from Vasil . . ." Jenny patted his hand, dabbed her eyes with a tissue, and laughed, quietly, just a sort of smile with sound, really. "Well, you know."

When Naum was at the seminary, the old monk Father Vasily

used to tell them stories. He'd been a priest in the old country. He lost his wife and children in the war. He came to America and helped found the seminary and the monastery. Father Vasily had been Naum's confessor.

The old monk, Father Vasily, said that as a child he fell into a big pot of boiling water. His mother rushed him to the church, where the priest held him by the elbow and dipped him in the blessed fountain. His elbow, where the priest had held him, even in his old age, looked boiled, but not the rest of him, even when they'd exhumed him.

Naum remembered one night at the seminary, coming home from an overnight job, just before dawn in the cold snowy dark, the locals told him it was so slippery on the mountain he had to cross, so slippery that you couldn't lie down on it . . .

Naum worked the overnight as a security guard six days a week to support his family and was so grateful that he and his old Jeep had made it home, that he went to the church to kiss the doors and thank God.

In the woods by the monastery church, deer, skunk, squirrels, raccoons, birds, and a black bear stood all together in Naum's headlights, and in the middle, the old monk, Father Vasily. Naum panicked and hit the horn. The animals went slowly away.

Naum thought the old man was senile, or confused, and had wandered out and couldn't get back in. Reassuring Father Vasily everything was okay, he led the quiet old man back to his cell, not realizing till many years later the thing he had witnessed, and what an idiot he had been.

One of the stories old Father Vasily loved to tell was this. He told it many times. Perhaps he thought the day might come when they would remember and find it refreshing and salutary to the soul.

A brother came to see Abba Macarios the Egyptian and said to him, "Abba, give me a word, that I may be saved."

So the old man said, "Go to the cemetery and abuse the dead."

The brother went there, abused them and threw stones at them; then he returned and told the old man about it.

The latter said to him, "Didn't they say anything to you?"

He replied, "No."

The old man said, "Go back tomorrow and praise them." So the brother went away and praised them, calling them apostles, saints, and righteous men. He returned to the old man and said to him, "I have complimented them."

And the old man said to him, "Did they not answer you?"

The brother said no.

The old man said to him, "You know how you insulted them and they did not reply, and how you praised them and they did not speak; so you too if you wish to be saved must do the same and become a dead man. Like the dead, take no account of either the scorn of men or their praises, and you can be saved."

A pitcher of water. Returning from the grave of Vasil Vasili, Naum rinsed his hands thoroughly, splashed his face, and rinsed the perfume, praise, and lipstick from his beard before entering again into their home. On the porch of the parish house, a pitcher. His Greta had placed it there. He went in and put the envelope on their kitchen table.

One Eye Open

———

IT WAS SNOWING PRETTY GOOD the day Lizzie's baby died.
Her family tried their best, but they had their own lives.

Mom and Pop were still young and good-looking.

Lived in different towns.

"When's it gonna be my turn?" *That* parental philosophy.

Mostly bought the kid off once she hit a certain age.

Old lipstick Grandma was there, comforting the delivery-room nurse.

Nobody knew who to be mad at.

The little guy was premature.

Swaddled stillborn in a receiving blanket.

One eye open. The other closed.

One eye open to what *eye has not seen*.

One closed to *our plight*.

Wearing a newborn beanie in a hospital bassinette.

There was a lot of crying.

After the prayer, Father Naum left the delivery room.

He went to see the Orthodox motel owner.

He'd taken Lizzie there the night before.

There was no room at the local teen shelter.

Family hadn't wanted her in their space that close to delivery.

Gus's was the only place Naum knew Lizzie might stay put.

He had no choice.

When Naum asked his old friend Gus about the possibility of a partial refund of the week's rent paid in advance—after all, she'd only been in the room a matter of hours before the ambulance arrived—Gus looked the old priest in the face from behind the counter and pointed behind his head to the writing on the wall.

ABSOLUTELY NO REFUNDS.

The looked at each other, not long.

"Okay," Naum said. "You're sure?"

Gus pointed again.

There was nothing to say.

Outside there were snow-coated stone squares on either side of the bottom steps, each of equal height and density. In summer they would have held a pot of red geraniums high enough to catch your eye.

At that moment in God's time, the snow-covered squares looked to Naum like Lambs on the diskos prior to Liturgy and Presanctified. He traced the IC XC – NI KA and a cross in the middle of each with his bare finger.

Down the road there was a vacant lot, and not knowing why, Naum went and stood with his face against the sky and let it snow in his eyes.

When it comes to living the Gospel, Naum thought, "I always like to give the Orthodox first crack." This was his practice.

He stared heavenward. The snow and the sky were becoming indistinguishable. They swirled together. He was mesmerized.

Liquefied memories, not tears, seeping through his lashes like the melting snow.

Once, he called Anchorage, Alaska, and asked the Orthodox priest there for help getting a trafficked kid home to her family back there. "Is she Orthodox?"

It went back and forth and nowhere.

The Catholic priest in Anchorage bought the ticket out of his own pocket.

Naum thought of another time, when Anastasia, a young Orthodox woman, died. Naum had known the family. They were among the faithful at Saint Alexander the Whirling Dervish Orthodox Church for many years. When the family moved away, they helped build an English-language mission in their new town, but the priest of the mission was laid off from his job as a prison chaplain and had to leave. So there were no services and no priest at the English-language mission.

During Anastasia's yearlong illness prior to her death, Naum made the sixty-mile drive to commune her once a week. He tried to comfort her husband, Viktor, who was Catholic, and her parents, Oscar and Marlene, faithful Orthodox people. The children, Christine and Gabriel, fourteen and sixteen, had both been baptized in the Orthodox Church.

Ten miles from Anastasia's home was a large, prosperous Orthodox church, but none of the services were in English. Naum and young Father Gregory, the pastor of the large nearby parish, had been friends for many years. They'd served together many times—weddings, Liturgies, baptisms, and funerals.

For the sake of Anastasia's family, for proximity and convenience, for comfort at such a time, Anastasia's funeral would be held there, at young Father Gregory's parish.

"Father?" The priest Gregory's voice was tentative on the line.

"Yes, what's wrong, Father?" Naum said.

"We have a problem." Father Gregory could've cried. "Our new bishop is insisting any priest outside his metropolis must have formal documentation from his bishop, copies of his ordination papers, sent to our bishop, confirming that he is in good canonical standing, and written permission from his own bishop to serve, and then another letter giving permission from our bishop to serve in any one of his parishes."

"Father," Naum said, "the day after tomorrow is the burial."

Gregory was helpless. "I know," he said. "I pleaded with him. I told him you'd been ahead of me at seminary and introduced me in the area when I was new, and that we'd served together many times. That you communed regularly when you were a student at our seminary. But he wouldn't budge. I am so sorry, Father."

Naum called the family. It was true he'd recently had a minor surgery. "I'm in too much pain to serve," he lied. "But I will come and stand with you," Naum told Viktor, Anastasia's husband.

But Viktor was furious. Her parents too. Only the children spoke to Naum at the funeral service. He did not stay for the memorial meal. They never answered his calls or letters. They never spoke to him again.

Standing in the snowy lot, Naum recalled the summer before, fifteen Russian teens were tricked into coming to America. They were drugged. They were exploited sexually. They managed to escape the owner of an amusement park who had lured them from their hometown of Yekaterinburg, where the tsar and his family had been murdered.

"Father Naum." Karl, a non-Orthodox friend, called Naum and explained. "I saw them huddled by a dumpster in the Walmart parking lot. I have them in my basement."

After many calls to the Orthodox community, only a poor working Russian priest from Brooklyn offered what little he had to help.

Ninety-year-old Rabbi Aaron from Temple Emanu-El across from Naum's parish, his grandparents had hidden behind the gravestones in the Jewish cemetery as mounted Cossacks carried out the pogrom in their village. Rabbi organized the Jewish American Veterans of Foreign Wars. They housed and fed the Russian kids in the synagogue and paid for the young people to return home to Yekaterinburg.

Naum was shivering now. He was thinking of a seminar featuring Kyriacos Markides, the author of *The Mountain of Silence*. It was to be held in a non-Orthodox venue, a venerable old fieldstone women's monastery.

"Not only is it large, and in a quiet, beautiful setting, with old trees and plenty of parking, but the nuns are so excited. They've read the book, they've advertised and told all their supporters, and they promise there will be crowds of non-Orthodox inquirers." Our Deborah, who was professor of religion at the local community college, had invited Professor Markides from the University of Maine. She told Naum, "And the nuns have waived the fee, *and* they're providing a full meal for us, gratis." Deborah was so excited. She said, "Please, Father, let the Orthodox Brotherhood know."

The Orthodox Brotherhood was offended by the non-Orthodox venue. Naum couldn't believe the Orthodox Clergy

Brotherhood had organized a boycott of Professor Markides' talk.

He stood there blinking in the snow. Then his cell phone rang.

"Okay," Gus said, "I'll give you your money."

For a minute, everything was still.

Naum said, "You sure, Gus?"

"*Malista.*" Indeed. Gus said, "She had the baby?"

"Stillborn," Naum said.

Gus hung up.

The snow was stopping. It was time to get back to the work.

"Okay, Lord," Naum prayed. "Still hope."

Naum's words condensed in the cold air and fell to the ground like icy teardrops from the steam while the breath of his prayer rose above his head like a whisper in the vapor and ascended with the little guy, encompassed now by angels, swaddled in the receiving blanket, one eye open to what *eye has not seen*, one eye closed to *our plight*, three times the priest breathing the Cross over the icon of his stillness in the newborn baptismal bassinette.

"Pray for us, blessed, pray for us, little man, pray to God for us, perfect icon, blessed child."

Simply Delicious

———•———

GIVEN THAT SHE WAS PICTURESQUE and informed of the axiomatic certainty that if one owned a hat, one ought to wear a hat, it followed naturally that Carol's *collection de chapeaux* did not include a bonnet, beret, cap, or cloche. Picture-frame hats for an axiomatically picturesque girl, was Carol's maxim, and a different color every day.

The women of Saint Alexander the Whirling Dervish Orthodox Church secretly loved Carol. The women of the parish also secretly wanted to wrap her hat around her head and beat her with raw filo dough.

"How does a woman her age still have a figure like that?" That's what Bernice wanted to know.

"Well," Ramona said, "not all of us have had children, have we?" Ramona immediately felt bad. She said, "Then again, maybe she can't. Poor thing."

"Poor thing, my Aunt Matilda! Maybe thank goodness she doesn't have children. Not everybody's cut out to raise kids. Then again, who knows?" said Bernice. "And besides, look who's talking. Ramona, even with your two, you still look like a girl."

"At least her head is covered when she comes to church," Madeline added.

Neither Carol nor her picture-frame hat had been seen in church for a long time. But recently, the women of the Teuta Ladies' Baking Society noticed Carol having long, tearful sessions with the priest. It seemed he always had someone nearby, just out of hearing range, when he met with anyone. Even with tradesmen, like Schmidt the baker; even with other priests.

The Village Thrift was an eclectic jumble of what Carol called *gently used*, pre-owned designer jewelry and vintage women's clothing. She would accept no less, outright purchase or on consignment, at her Spruce Street shop down by the riverfront. It had a stylish green awning over the wide front bay window and a compact, cozy balcony outside the second-floor apartment where she lived.

Late spring and all summer long, even into early autumn, the iron-railed balcony provided Carol the perfect perch to sit unobserved and review the spectacle of fashion-forward trendies parading past the shop to Spruce Street Harbor Park, the hammock-filled haven on the Delaware River waterfront.

Note to self: Obviously, it bothered her. She posted it on the refrigerator door. *Dear Carol, church people? In here? In my store? I never see them. As much as I donate in support from my proceeds, you'd think they'd pop their heads in my Village Thrift from time to time.*

Why didn't they come? Embarrassment. A simple, unadorned, one-word explanation that no one would admit. To be seen to covet *designer* labels, hundred-dollar shoes at half the cost, movie-star hats, and debutante dresses at a discount price?

Not our gals. Besides, the ladies thought, where would they wear such extravagant things? Supermarket shopping? Sitting with their husbands in front of the TV watching *Jeopardy*, eating supper from a TV tray and shouting answers at the screen, or an occasional ladies' side-door entrance to the dining room at Shooky's Taproom for cabbage and beer night? Sawdust and shuffleboard didn't exactly lend itself to gently used Gucci.

Arguments about Carol and her clothing went back and forth every time the ladies of the Teuta Ladies' Baking Society gathered to bake for the upcoming ethnic festivals. Kurabia, Bernice's specialty, butter cookies covered in powdered sugar; byrek, filo dough rolled thin and filled with spinach or goat cheese, what the Greeks called spanakopita; *tullumba*, pieces of syrup-drenched fried dough, and our own version of what people called *baklava*, and with real butter—the girls baked it all.

Madeline cleaned the counters, and before going home, each meeting was finished with the lighting of the tabletop censer, prayers, and baking the meshe.

After, during the final cleanup, Bernice said, "That's all well and good, but our Carol is no Queen Teuta."

No one disputed the Ladies' Society's namesake, Queen Teuta, and her risqué pirate-queen reputation. She no doubt had dressed and done as she pleased, designer be damned. After all, she was Teuta, the warrior queen of Illyria who defied even Rome. But when it came to church, modest dress and head-coverings went without saying. Carol coming to church dressed like a one-woman pirate-queen festival? Madeline said, "Oh, bo bo!"

Tertullian said that in his lifetime, less than two hundred years after our Master's Ascension, women in the church communion at Corinth were still following the teaching of Saint Paul, who planted the church in Corinth and had appealed to the women to cover their heads.

"Says so on my smartphone," Ramona told the girls. Petite, wiry Ramona. People said she still looked like a girl. Close enough to forty to stick out her tongue and touch it.

And damn if it didn't perturb the older women when they thought she was ignoring them as they talked, all the time she spent poking that phone.

Kurabia, the crescent-shaped butter cookies covered in powdered sugar, were the only item in the Teuta Ladies' Baking Society repertoire that consistently sold out, the only thing that saved Ramona and her phone. As a girl she had perfected a recipe from her mother's mother that would have melted the tricks of Kusheri Nastradin, the famous trickster, right off the tip of his storytelling tongue.

Perpetual-Motion Mona, "like a fish who never stops swimming" was what Ramona's husband, Thomo, called her. He said, "My girl's oblivious to who's perturbed or not."

At the same time Ramona was quick to let her eight-year-old twins, Mona and Julian, know, "Quit poking that phone while I'm talking to you."

Then there was Madeline. If you saw her creamy brown skin and her crispy brown eyes, you would have no trouble believing they named that cookie—butter, flour, and sugar, lots of sugar—after our Madeline.

Madeline never missed a Bible study. She had a son she named Clement. "Not after the one who went to Rome and worked with Saint Paul, who wrote the letter that used to be in the Bible.

Not that Clement. My Clement is named after Saint Clement the bishop of Alexandria who says, 'Go to church decent.' So I keep this, right here, in my pocket." She dusted the flour from her hands and shook out the gauzy white veil with the delicate cross embroidery.

Bernice said, "My cousin by marriage, Hawwa, the Egyptian woman married to my cousin Eddie, Two-Beer Eddie, remember her? She keeps the veil in her pocket too. Me? I just look at Holy Mother. That's all I need to know. When I was a kid, all I wore was blue and purple, 'cause that's what she wore, in the icons."

Bernice had the resolve and serious demeanor typical of many of our Orthodox women, women Solzhenitsyn called strong, resolute, and creative. She always wore a plain dress, blue or purple, and simple solid shoes.

Her glasses looked like Army issue. Everything about Bernice was functional and made for work. "Me, wear a pantsuit? Never. And to church? Do I look like Carol?" she said, looking around to make sure Father Naum, still sitting with the sobbing Carol, was at an earshot-safe distance.

Ramona said, "Anyone ask the priest? About head coverings?"

That caused the counters to get floured maybe a little more than they should have. They looked over at Naum and wondered if he had heard. It looked like he and Carol were just finishing their talk.

Father Naum and Carol came to where the ladies were working, and when Naum started in, Ramona said, "Yep, he heard."

Prostitutes. The Teuta women couldn't believe he was saying it in church. Even there in the kitchen where they were baking the holy bread.

What surprised them even more? Carol.

Carol was actually sitting with them, in her pantsuit, wearing her hat, her dangling gold earrings, painted nails, ringed fingers, dabbing her mask runny with tears after her talk with Naum, asking for coffee. "Black, please, demitasse, with a saucer."

Bernice brought it. She forgot to ask Father if he wanted a coffee. He just went on talking like priests do.

Carol said, "Napkin?"

Bernice brought a stack.

Carol said "thank you" from her perch on the high stool and dusted the flour from the counter, dusted it to the floor with her napkin.

"You're welcome, Carol." Bernice went away and returned with a dustpan and broom.

Naum was saying, "In Corinth there was a popular temple to Aphrodite, popular with visiting seamen and locals too, popular because of the temple prostitutes. In AD 20, Strabo called them *pornai*. These poor women were probably slaves bought by men and given to the temple as some kind of religious offering. Bizarre to us. And it is."

The women of the impromptu Bible study straightened their aprons and studied the utensils in their laps.

There they were, all seated on stools around the counter where the holy bread was rising under clean dishcloths reserved only for proofing the bread.

When Naum finally sat down, he looked at the mounds of dough under the colorful towels and said, "It's always good to have a meshe rising."

Madeline didn't like the fact that Naum didn't have a cup in front of him. She took his cup, the one with his name on it, filled it with coffee, and set it in front of Father Naum.

He sipped it and said, "Ah, the keeper of her brother's cup." And went on. "Well, you can imagine Saint Paul, trying his best to plant the vine in Corinth, where this temple is booming and the wives of the locals are going wild, bleaching their hair blonde and running around Corinth naked from the waist up, protesting their husbands always being in the temple.

"And our Christian reputation precedes us, no doubt. This new religion, outlaw atheists who won't burn incense to the emperor, sex-crazed agape-feast cannibals eating the body and blood of a man. So is it any wonder Saint Paul advises, let our women be covered, to distinguish us and maybe keep a low profile, even?"

Bernice whispered to Ramona, "You had to go and ask."

"But mainly," Naum said, "it's us for others, and them for us, that we dress modestly, cover ourselves. The clothes set a tone. I ask myself, in church or not, am I in harmony with God's liturgy for the eucharistic life, or am I a liturgical distraction?"

Carol had finished her coffee. She said, "Father, ladies, I am grateful for your time. Thank you for including me, but I have to go and open the store."

She took out three one-hundred-dollar bills and gave them to Bernice. "May I please make a donation to the Teuta Society?" Carol said, "If I can't be here helping, girls—I'm not a good baker—then I can at least do something. And I want you to know, I pray for all of you, and your families, by name, every day. And I ask your prayers too."

Bernice was a little sad when she said, "Thank you, Carol."

GOOD PASTORAL WORK TAKES TIME. Building a relationship, planting, cultivating, and finding just the right place for new shoots in the garden is not easy, and it doesn't produce fruit overnight.

Naum had been accompanying Carol. Walking with her in the desert. Pointing home.

He'd learned about Carol's father—"My father had the reputation as a good priest back in the old country"—and about the sacrifices of her mother, "when she would say she wasn't hungry and give me her food in the camp, during her last days when she told me, 'God's love in me for you is stronger than the weakness of my body.'"

The family fleeing in a crowded boxcar on the last train west one Sunday after Liturgy, a parishioner knocking, warning them during supper, with only one hour's notice. All they could carry bundled in the dining-room tablecloth. Carrying their little girl, Carol, frightened and confused.

How they were captured, and what young Carol and her family suffered in the camps.

"My father never once said, 'Where is God?'" Carol said.

Carol was a long time recovering.

She told Naum, "You have no idea of the viciousness, the depravity people are capable of inflicting on one another, or the extent of pain, anguish, and hopelessness the human body is capable of feeling.

"When we were liberated, American soldiers—boys, they were just boys—stood there crying when they saw us. Naked. No hair.

Skin clinging to bones. We wanted food. They gave us cigarettes and water. Even the chocolate bars they wanted to give, they couldn't. The doctors told us it would be too much, it would kill us. We'd have to come back to life slowly. I never found my father or my mother."

With her family gone, she led a solitary, lonely life after arriving in America. Every night she told God, "I am so lonely, and I am afraid to tell you what I am truly feeing. I am afraid to offend you, God."

She was afraid to go to church. She said, "The things I heard people in the camps say about God, what they really thought about the Church, and priests, the things I saw religious people do just to survive, the things people did to my mother, to each other, and to me."

A friend suggested she needed to get out of her own head, find some companionship. Go to an online dating site and arrange a date.

When Carol arrived at a downtown restaurant to meet her prospective match, it was the well-known priest of a local Orthodox parish—a single man, but nonetheless.

It affected her so deeply, it took Naum three years of pastoral patience and listening for Carol to consider returning to Communion.

Even a shriveled seed, Naum said, if carefully nurtured, can come back, a little at a time.

———————

SUNDAY COMMUNION TIME. Father Naum was glad there was no comment or commotion when the Andy Warhol color portrait of Marilyn Monroe approached the chalice in her hat. She was a picture, indeed. Didn't matter. Father was just glad Carol had found her direction home.

When he communed her, Carol said, "Delicious, simply delicious."

Naum was a bit startled, but not offended. He knew it was just the beginning of Carol's being home. Her healthy memory would return, he had no doubt. She had to come back to life slowly.

Naum was known for telling the people he served, "Let me make it easy for you. You work hard enough. I will come to you. We can meet and walk home together. I know the way."

Naum knew our Master met Saint Photini, the Samaritan woman, where she was. He met her at the well, with all she was and with all she had to say. Photini began to know Him because He knew her.

The Father recognized both sons as prodigal, and while they were still a long way off, he ran to meet them in their recklessness. The younger son prodigal with worldly blessings, the other heedless of the spiritual blessing he mindlessly squandered.

Being picturesque and informed of the axiomatic certainty that if one owned a hat, one ought to wear a hat, a smiling Carol, dressed all in lavender, turned from the chalice, daintily nibbling the antidoron, made the cross, and nodded to each of her sisters of the Teuta Ladies' Baking Society as she made her way up the aisle and returned to her place in the pews.

"I love your hat," Bernice, in her plain dress, whispered as Carol went by.

Carol touched her hand. "I have one at the shop, Bernice, and a dress this color too."

"It's becoming my favorite color," Bernice said.

They embraced, and Carol said, "Why not wear them while we can?"

The choir sang, "Oh, taste and see, oh, taste and see that the Lord is good, that the Lord is good."

————————

IT WAS ALL UNDONE, less than an hour later, in a single act of well-meaning intervention by someone who thought it their prerogative to usurp the pastoral obedience of the priest.

Most other folks were happy at coffee hour.

Carol was standing in the deacon's door, not inside the altar, just at the open door, so Naum could hear as he consumed the Gifts. Deacon Dionysios was there to direct her.

Naum asked Carol to please pray the prayers of thanksgiving after returning from all those years away from Communion.

He had shown her the prayers of preparation, she had said them faithfully the night before, and Naum wanted her to know about the prayers of thanksgiving too, the prayers said after receiving Holy Communion.

The person—man or woman, Naum wouldn't say—said, "Does it matter?" The interloper loudly chastised Carol for being a woman in the altar.

The deacon could only watch and shake his head.

Carol left sobbing and shaking, the prayer book left open on the analogion by the icon of the Theotokos.

Naum advised the canon expert to pray for Carol and assured the judge of other persons that he or she would surely be standing with Carol and answerable at the judgment if Carol did not return to Christ.

Naum communed God's people, as much as it was in his power to do so.

At the next session of the Teuta Ladies' Baking Society, Ramona opened the meeting reading the Morning Prayer of the Last Elders of Optina from her phone. When she put her phone away she said, "I can hardly answer for my own sins. But I've been more and more sad since Sunday."

Madeline looked at the girls and said, "Our sister's keeper?"

Bernice stood, untying her apron. "Any of you girls want to take a ride on the forty-seven, accompany me to the Village Thrift? Carol says she's got a lavender hat and dress down there might look good on my big *koka-dru*." Her big wooden head.

"And I've baked two dozen of my kurabia," Ramona said, "especially for her."

It was voted to postpone the meeting, and while the meshes were rising under the colorful cloths, to take the 47 trolley down to Spruce Street, to sit and have coffee on the pleasant iron-railed balcony overlooking the stylish green awning above the wide front bay window, outside the second-floor apartment of Carol's Village Thrift.

Option One

—•—

MY FRIEND CANDACE goes to an Orthodox church, you know, like in *My Big Fat Greek Wedding*, the movie.

Anyhow, there's a guy there, at the church, hitting on her.

Now what's awkward is, my friend Candace's mother, Athena, and her father, George? They go to that same church, Saint Alexander's, the one across the street from Temple Emanu-El.

Mira and Panteleimon go there too. Candace calls them Mira and Pandi. They're old friends of her parents.

Candace says the four old folks—Athena and George, Mira and Pandi—have been hanging out for years. They do everything together, couples, you know, old people stuff. Senior bus trips. Casino junkets. Tours of the Liberty Bell—not the racetrack in the Northeast, not *that* Liberty Bell, but the old cracked bell downtown, that's the one they go see. God knows why. They line up with the coupons they clip for the early-bird specials at the all-you-can-eat Trolley Car Diner buffet over on Frankford Avenue. They even got Pandi to fly out to Vegas, and Pandi *hates* to fly, but he loved the buffets out there.

Candace says her father's buddy Pandi looks a lot like the

Queen of Hearts in his Mummers getup. The two old buds, Pandi and George, been marching in the Mummers Parade for forty years. More maybe.

When they were kids, before they joined the Fishtown String Band, Pandi and George used to head down to the open-air huckster market on Second Street with their Radio Flyer wagon with the wood-slat sides and salvage as many solid wood crates from the fire pile as they could and sell them to people, nickel apiece, to stand on to see the string bands over the crowd.

Mira, Pandi's wife, she loves to tease Pandi in the church hall after Liturgy about his Queen of Hearts costume. She sings that Juice Newton song to him. She has to take her teeth out to do it though, and the way she lisps makes everybody at the coffee-hour table laugh even more.

But Pandi puts up with it 'cause it's Mira sews his Mummers costume so he can march with the Fishtown String Band playing "O! Dem Golden Slippers" on his 1951 five-string banjo.

George, Candace's father? He sews his own Mummery getup, George the Joker, who else? And you can imagine how they look, these two, the sunrise headgear, feathers and bangles, face makeup, sequins and beads, swigging flasks between numbers, out there on parade, oblivious to the freezing cold. Happy old geezers, neither of 'em over five foot six, one more time, doing the Mummers strut up Broad Street on New Year's Day like a couple o' tipsy peacocks—George the Joker clocking his glockenspiel doing the Two Street strut, shuffling to keep up with banjo-picking Pandi, the Queen of Hearts.

Now everybody in the neighborhood knows veteran Mummer-wives like Athena and Mira ain't never gonna be standing out there in the cold watching the parade anymore like when they were young and had to, damn thing drags on over eight hours. Besides, perfect excuse, it's Saint Basil's Liturgy that morning, so after church, Mira and Athena go home, get supper ready, cabbage and ham, and watch the whole thing on TV, but never at Mira's.

Mira, Pandi's wife, smokes. Smokes ain't the word. Candace says her house smells like a bar in a Marlboro commercial. "Poor Mira," Candace tells me. "She lost the tips of two fingers 'cause of smoking. Diabetes. Little too much butter cake and Ramona's kurabia cookies from the Teuta Ladies' Baking Society didn't help either. Had to get thicker glasses too, Mira. Same color silver, the glasses, as her hair."

At church, their priest—Candace says his name is Naum—he stands up one day and tells them, "No more smoking at coffee hour in the church hall as of today."

"And they do it," she says.

I say, "Wow, Candace, I'm impressed. That's some authority. I don't know if even Rabbi could pull *that* off."

Candace says, "Nah, Jilly. Took him two years going house to house of all the smokers, drinking bad coffee and letting the dog smell him, and Mira was the last holdout."

"Really? How'd it happen?"

"Not through reason or logic, Jill," Candace says.

On his last visit, Mira asks the priest, Father Naum, "Hey, Father, why's my twins not coming ta church anymore?"

The priest says, "Doctor Dara stopped bringing them."

Mira's not happy. She calls her daughter, Dara.

Her daughter the doctor tells her, "Mom, I'm not subjecting

Karla and Leslie to all that cigarette smoke."

Mira stops smoking, at least at church.

Now apparently, over in the vestibule at the church, they have these big wide sandboxes on stands. Candace says they're nice-looking too. Candace's father, George, and his old buddy Pandi get together in Pandi's woodshop in the garage and do some pretty amazing finish carpentry.

I say, "Sandboxes?"

She tells me, "Yeah, Jilly. We go to the candle counter, they call it a pangar, it's in the vestibule, we call that the narthex. Pandi and my father built the pangar too, like a big counter that holds all the candles. And they're these beeswax candles, you oughta smell 'em. Smell like honey. My father actually makes them at home in our cellar.

"He has a double boiler," Candace says, "dips the wicks until he gets the thickness he wants. Hangs them over a long wooden dowel rod. Three different sizes. Three different prices. They raise a lot of money for the church. The people stop at the pangar, buy the candles, then they go in front of the icons that sit on stands with angled tops, stands called analogions. Pandi and my dad built them too.

"The analogions are kind of slanted podiums on high legs. They sit them near the sandboxes that are up on belly-level stilts, the people light their candle, stick the candle in the sand, make the cross, say a prayer, and kiss the icon."

I told Candace I like candles. Just not scented ones. Them, I can't take. Beeswax candles, though. I wish we had them where I go.

Candace says her priest told the people Jesus was the light in a dark world and the darkness won't overcome His love, or something like that. And the candles do double duty. That's what she said. One, they make a nice light, especially at the night services. And two, they represent Jesus, the Light of the world.

"Makes sense," I said. What else was I gonna say? I'm Jewish.

So, a little off track here, I get it, but her folks, George and Athena, starting to look like twins, to me they did. You know how some old people get, where you can't tell if the man's a man or the woman's a woman? Same haircut. Same stretch pants. Same orthopedic shoes. Both with the wraparound laser-blocking sunglasses Martians wear on the moon.

I mean, geez, good thing Athena carries a handbag or I'd have a heck of a time tellin' 'em apart, 'cept from the back. George with the ponytail hanging off the back of his bald head and he even wears an earring. A guy his age with an earring.

Plus, their voices start to sound the same too. Athena, Candace's mom, sings in the choir, and the choir director forbade George to even sing anywhere in church except in the narthex when he's selling candles back there at the pangar where nobody can hear his high soprano singing except himself.

Candace, my friend, is some kind of professor, maybe Gender Studies or something like that. She looks like a professor too. Wild hair. Got the *I gotta be smart—Karl Marx is my uncle—power to the people* round-lens tortoiseshell glasses thing going on. And I'm not saying the woman *ain't* smart. She is. Smarter than me anyway.

Street savvy though? That's a whole 'nother story. I worry about Candace when it comes to surviving in the real world, like on her nighttime subway ride home from university.

I been going to Krav Maga over at the Temple for a couple o' years learning self-defense and tried to get her to come. She blew me off. "Yeah, maybe after finals." Least she knew what it was. "That Israeli martial arts karate?" she says.

And when it comes to fashion sense, my color-blind Candace, sliding out every morning with her mismatched Birkenstock socks, corduroy to the floor, beads on her knees, round little 1960s vintage protest pins on her home-knit lopsided vest, got the ethnic brain squeezer beanie making her woolly hair spring out both sides like the shearer missed a spot with the electric clippers. She's happy though.

Candace goes to the priest and says, "One of the men in the parish is hitting on me. It makes me uncomfortable, and I don't feel safe when I'm in church."

She called it microagression.

Me? I'd've decked his ass.

The priest asks what anyone would ask. "You feel comfortable telling me who?"

My friend Candace says she made a mistake. She told her father's best bud Pandi she thinks he looks real cute as the Queen of Hearts. I don't think Pandi took it the right way.

Candace tells the priest, "He invites me to lunch and tells me he's quite aware of our mutual attraction and even though he's married, and older, there's no reason why we can't add a little joy to each other's lives."

Then, you're not gonna believe this one, Pandi tells Candace, his good friend George's daughter, "Not that I need Viagra, but I got plenty and nothing at home to do with it."

I would've told this joker exactly what to do with it, but not

Professor Candace.

When Candace tells the priest it's the Queen of Hearts, the woodworking, candle-selling, Mummer-strutting, banjo-playing church elder, her father's best bud Pandi, the priest turns red in the face with embarrassment. Or maybe he was pissed off. When it comes to priests, Candace says, it's hard to tell.

According to Candace, this priest wants to run right out and confront the guy, but Candace grabs him by the back of the collar, so to speak.

They sit there, Candace and this Father Naum, looking at each other in astonished silence, each one doing their own interpersonal permutation calculations in the front pew of the church after the Liturgy, and they can hear the two couples, old friends, George and Athena, and Mira and randy Pandi, out there laughing at coffee hour in the church hall.

Candace said the priest really was pissed. That okay ta say?

"No, Jilly," Candace tells me. "It's not."

Maybe that's what she meant by microaggression.

The priest wanted to kick this guy out, discreetly, of course, you know, like tell him privately, either you tell your wife the truth or make up a story why you're not coming to church anymore, but whatever you do, you're gonna apologize to Candace and come to your senses or you're gone.

Okay. The priest calms down and tells Candace, "If it's okay with you, I'd like both of us to take a week. I have someone I trust I'd like to run this by, without names—protect your confidentiality, of course. And we'll talk again next Sunday."

You know who he goes to see? Corrine! That dark-skinned woman who runs the teen homeless shelter, the one with the

PhD and the gap-toothed killer smile? Yep. Her. I thought he'd be going to see his bishop or some older priest or some wise old monk or nun, or rabbi. The priest and our rabbi hang out and drink tea at least once a week. Love to be a fly on the wall there.

But nope. He goes to Corinne, that's her name, a no-nonsense, practical person who knows her way around human nature. She tells him, "The woman who was hit on? She don't need you. She can handle it. Tell her, don't worry about this guy. Don't play into his old man fantasy and give credence to his whacked-out crap. Tell her, get used to dealing with idiots. If it's the girl I'm thinking about, the professor"—How Corrine guessed? Naum had no idea—"that woman can hold her own." Corrine tells the priest, "She doesn't need a coalition or a church committee. Now, Naum, my friend, go back and tell her, this is what to do."

The minute Corinne said it, the priest knew it was true.

Parish softball games, he'd seen Candace swing a bat.

The next week Candace went to Pandi privately. She says, "I made Father Naum aware that you had a serious temporary lapse in judgment when you invited me to lunch and made your bizarre proposal. Suppose my father did that to your daughter, Doctor Dara?"

Candace says Pandi almost danced "O Dem Golden Slippers" out the door when he heard the priest knew.

She told him, "So here's the deal. You've got two options here. Option one. You apologize. We drop it and never mention it again.

"Or, option two, you persist in your delusions, and the priest and I go together to your wife, Mira, and tell her your daughter, Doctor Dara, needs to yank your prescription for Viagra and refer you for therapy."

I heard later when Pandi told the priest he had a mental Mummers misstep, the priest told him, "It happens when the golden slippers start to get old. Do yourself a favor and come to confession," and from what Candace says, Pandi did, more than once.

Candace said he was a good boy after she set him straight. Maybe a little ashamed to look at her. The friendship with her parents kind of cooled down. Pandi lost his interest in woodworking and Mummery, sat in the house with Mira and took up smoking.

———

I'LL TELL YOU WHAT THE SAD THING WAS, for me. I never got to meet Mira or Pandi.

Mira went not long after him. Less than a week apart. I never saw a funeral with two coffins. Then again I never lit a candle and put it in a sandbox.

The way the whole thing hit me at their funeral, the temple layout of that little church, the incense, the curtain over the door, the seven-branched candle, the cantor up there chanting this kind of mystical lament, was all so familiar, I'd swear I was in Temple.

Next thing I knew, there I was, alone in the back of the church with my beeswax candle, getting ready to stick it in the sand, make the cross, and kiss the icon of Jesus out there in the vestibule.

Well, maybe not. 'Cause up behind me creeps George the Joker, Candace's father, there behind *me*, up against *me* at the sandbox in the vestibule.

What's that line about not suffering fools gladly? It happened so fast, I guess I just reacted. I don't think I coulda ever kicked a Mummer if I'da thought about it. I sorta remember saying that Joker line while he was lying there on the floor looking up at me: "I used to be a people person, but people like you ruined that for me."

I felt bad. I put out my hand to help him up and offered to help him look around for his earring while I was explaining what I meant by Krav Maga.

Eventually I found his earring rolled over in front of the pangar. When I handed it to him I think it was his pride hurt more than anything.

After, I went in and sat with Candace toward the back. I thought about it during the service and decided damn if I'm telling Candace where I planted that beeswax candle, or that her father did the same as Pandi and took option one.

The Procession

FATHER NAUM USED TO SAY he'd never seen a U-Haul truck in a funeral procession. We all knew what that meant. You can't take it with you.

But we had to laugh. Urania—they called her Emma because most Americans had trouble saying *Urania*—well, in Emma's funeral procession there was a nephew who changed all that, an eccentric, lovable, goofy nephew named Xenakis Qeni.

Now a name like Urania was challenge enough. But growing up in an inner-city Philly neighborhood like Fishtown with a name like Xenakis Qeni?

Might incline you to think life at recess confined to the top of the monkey bars, winter and summer, in that rough-cracked blacktop schoolyard wouldn't be so pleasant, but not if you had a perspective on life like Xenakis Qeni.

Up there Xenakis felt safe. Safe from the bullies down below. "You better not come down, Naki," they'd warn.

And in good weather, nobody had a view of redheaded Henrietta Reese like Naki, trapped like a pole-sitter atop the monkey bars. Consolation enough, what Naki thought, seeing Henrietta bounce around the dodgeball circle. A daydream in a tight white blouse. Even after they were grown and she married that Catholic kid, Billy John Marco, and robbed her own wedding, Naki still dreamed of Henrietta.

The neighborhood boys got to calling him Naki Q. And in his early twenties, the summer he was on workman's comp from the putty factory—he'd fallen on his head climbing down from cleaning the three-story funnel—people said, *What's the difference whether it was the fall or breathing in the chemical solvent that did it?* Either way, everybody agreed, that accident was the reason Xenakis took on his new neighborhood persona as Q the Cop.

Out from behind telly-poles he'd jump when unsuspecting drivers passing through the neighborhood came to a halt at the stop sign on the corner of Lawrence and Norris.

Blue pants. Long-sleeved blue work shirt buttoned to the collar with his dead father's worn-out, double-wide black leather belt strung diagonally across his chest, sporting a Cracker Jack seven-point flimsy tin badge.

The flattened dime-store police cap down over his ears, Q the Cop took an official stand, hands on his hips over the Hopalong Cassidy cowboy holster with the Roy Rogers cap gun mounted proudly at his side.

Notebook in hand, sliding the pencil from behind his ear, wetting the lead with his tongue, Q the Cop would swagger to the driver's-side window.

"What's wrong, officer?"

The neighbors sitting on the steps across the street laughing.

Then the out-of-the-neighborhood driver would notice the plastic paraphernalia and Q's high-top, oversized white Chuck

Taylor sneakers and wave off Q the Cop in amused irritation, taillights disappearing across the trolley tracks on Fifth Street past John's Hofbrauhaus.

And damn if Urania's eccentric nephew Q the Cop could afford a car or get a ride to her funeral. He just didn't have what it took to own a car. But damn again if that was gonna stop Q the Cop. He got somebody to rent him a truck. A big orange-and-white ten-foot U-Haul truck. All he could afford. The empty truck rumbled along in the funeral procession, bouncing its way across the American Street railroad tracks and the uneven cobblestones, the barren cargo cabin echoing like the 47 trolley rolling through the Fifth Street tunnel, all the way to the grassy lawns of the Orthodox section in Oakland Graveyard.

Now, thanks to Naki Q, even for Father Naum it was hard not to smile whenever he got ready to deliver his famous line about never having seen a U-Haul truck in a funeral procession.

———•———

BUT THERE WAS ANOTHER PROCESSION that ranked high on the list of funerary motorcades at Saint Alexander the Whirling Dervish parish.

She came in on a Sunday after Liturgy.

Father Naum was in the altar. Deacon Dionysios, Georgie Yarrow, and Andreas Rolfess were reading the prayers of thanksgiving after Communion as Father consumed the Gifts at the table of oblation.

May Thy Holy Body be unto me for eternal life, and Thy precious Blood for the forgiveness of my sins, O Lord Jesus Christ, our God . . .

The men would alternate, each reading a prayer of

thanksgiving, until Father finished consuming the consecrated bread and wine that remained in the chalice after he'd distributed Holy Communion to the faithful at the Liturgy.

The prayers would continue until Father Naum finished cleansing the utensils and the chalice, and they ended in the traditional way with the deacon saying, "Lord have mercy, Lord have mercy, Lord have mercy. Father, give the blessing."

As Naum made the final blessing, there was a quiet knock on the deacon's door.

An unusually handsome young man dressed in a fine black cashmere overcoat, all in black—suit, tie, shoes, hat in hand—said to Georgie Yarrow at the deacon's door, "Please, sir, my mother would like to speak with the Father, if he has time." His English was perfect, as if he'd been to one of the better schools in England.

His mother had been waiting, sitting quietly in the pews, but when she heard the prayers of thanksgiving, she stood and remained standing, even when the prayers were finished and her son approached the deacon's door on the iconostasis.

She studied the long wall that screened the altar from the nave. A wide set of royal doors arched in the middle and was covered with a curtain that could be pulled to one side.

She knew church buildings were meant to face east, and she could see there were two deacon's doors on either side of the wide royal doors in the middle. Both deacon's doors were adorned with icons of archangels. The angel on the right side, the south door as she faced the icon screen, she knew was Gabriel. The other angel on the left, the north deacon's door, was the icon of the Archangel Michael.

Tatiana, that was her name, she loved the angels. Her husband had not been religious. He was older than she. He had a hundred ways to let her know God was a stranger in his house and that for his wife, Tatiana, church was not an option.

But from when she was a little girl, well, she had a good mother, Maria. The priest at home in her country knew their piety, mother Maria and daughter Tatiana. He used to say that the Kingdom within the heart of the mother was the bridal chamber that would give birth to the faith of the daughter.

Tatiana was the picture of elegance. Simple. Refined. Intelligent. A kind person. Father Naum had seen her occasionally in the back of the church, early on Sunday morning long before most people arrived, lighting many candles and filling the basket on the pangar with twenty-dollar bills.

Tatiana, for some reason, never stayed for Liturgy. Father had never known her to receive Holy Communion. He wondered, now, why she had come to see him.

Your place of origin, how you looked, your accent or clothing, what you did for a living never mattered to Naum. He just didn't seem to notice or put much stock in those things. Beneath the presentation there was a deeper person residing, and this was where relationship took place.

But Father Naum could not help noticing, Tatiana was so young and so innocently delicate. The prima donna of nesting *matryoshka* dolls, the astonishing one with the Fabergé face.

And the tall young man all in black, with the manners and bearing that Father thought made him either a gypsy or a son of the Romanov court, came to stand with his mother.

And Tatiana. The French silk Chanel black dress, her Saint

Laurent Chesterfield coat that overlaid her shoulders like a cape, black handbag, black shoes and stockings, black veil and hat. Hair so black and tightly pulled back. The minimal palette of the face so perfect and pale.

He, this young man, was her son? Was he too old for such a young mother? Was she not too young for a son that age? But no. It was so, however mathematically incalculable it may have seemed to Naum.

It struck Father Naum as no less incalculable that eyes so luminous and black—that so subtle a lisp, teeth so white, and accent so engaging—that a woman appearing so inwardly full of life as Tatiana should be appealing to him concerning death.

"Father, please, may I ask about funeral arrangements for my husband?"

Beneath the presentation there was a deeper person residing, and this was where relationship took place.

How did Father Naum know this?

Folktales and tunes are better unrecorded, better left to live participation and performance, and for Naum, knowing others was the same.

"I was a little boy once, a toddler who couldn't talk. I didn't care how my hair looked, what clothes I wore, or what people thought of me, and I had no qualms about running out the door and down the street naked." This was the only explanation Naum would offer.

Professor Candace told us it had something to do with pretension. For most of us, that explanation was like trying to tell which way the trolley ran by looking at the tracks.

Naum said to Tatiana, "Your son has a Belgravian accent."

"Plummy," said the young man. His name was Sergei. "Is what they call it at my school, a plummy accent."

Tatiana said, "I insisted we send him to school in England."

"And your husband agreed," Father stated.

Tatiana only smiled.

Father said, "I've seen you here, many times, lighting candles in front of the icon of Saint Matrona of Moscow."

"She was blind from birth and couldn't see the icons of the good people with whom she surrounded herself. I can see, but until I read the story of her life, I was blind to all the bad with which I had surrounded myself," said Tatiana.

Father Naum told Tatiana, "Your husband came here."

Sergei, the son, said, "Are you sure?" He was surprised, but Tatiana knew.

She said, "He came home very sad. You wouldn't take his money. He wanted to confess, but only if you would take his money."

Father said nothing. The money her husband had offered was such a large amount, it frightened the priest. Although he knew intellectually it was possible, he had never known so much money could actually be in the hands of one man until that morning before Liturgy.

Naum sensed the poor man had no idea that the exchange he was proposing and the conditions he attached to his offering would only increase his alienation from God and from others and become a further toxin to his soul.

The older women of the parish saw the man leave that morning. They were worried. "Did you hear his confession?" Zenaida asked.

Father told them the man had changed his mind. That was all he would say.

Fedya said, "I pray he doesn't change it again."

But Raskova had said, "I am glad not to be afraid for you, Father. This is a man taking violence in his way."

Then Father said to Tatiana, "It could be that after his burial, we might see you lighting candles here again."

Tatiana lowered her eyes.

———•———

THE DAY OF THE FUNERAL, Father Naum sent Xenakis Qeni out to the curb. He said, "Naki, do you have your badge with you?"

"Yes, Father," said Naki Q the Cop.

"Good. Go out and count the yellow cabs." Then he shouted after Naki, "And the men, too."

Naki made his way out through the crowd of men standing by the last row of pews and in the narthex, the same crowd Father Naum had to navigate to get into the altar.

Father had gone by, asking the men, "Please, brothers, if you could, please, for me, I'm too old and don't breathe well like you young fellows. Please, for your old cousin Naum, smoke outside."

And they did. The men, all wearing black leather jackets, leaning on the back walls. None sat in the pews, but they did lean over them like cowboys at a corral, all wearing pointy-toed shiny shoes, all with workman's caps stuffed in their pockets. To a man, they grinned and apologized. "Sure, Father, sure. No problem."

The undertakers were solemn in their studied workaday way as they wheeled the casket to the front of the church.

Tatiana and Sergei were the only family members there. They escorted the coffin into the church, Father Naum leading with the censer, chanting the prayers.

The coffin was opened, feet facing the altar, and Sergei placed an icon called the Descent into Hades, Christ at Pascha, in the hands of his father.

Tatiana kissed her husband. She trembled. Silent tears were on her face. She placed an icon of Saint Matrona on his breast.

Xenakis Qeni rang the bell.

Naum opened the curtain on the royal doors.

Mother and son, so close to each other, held hands on the lonely front bench, framed in the vacant legacy of empty pews left by the man in the brass-handled casket.

There was no chanter. No server. No choir or psalti.

Xenakis Qeni took off his police hat. He made sure the candles were lighted and that Father Naum had the censer when he needed it. He liked being an altar server. Father said he was good at it too.

Naum chanted alone, the petitions and the responses. He was used to it. He prayed all the prayers. Long ago his teachers had prepared him. *Know the services by heart,* they said, *but always have your book in your hand. These words are not your words. It is prideful to do otherwise.*

Naum couldn't help but look up from his book at the man in the coffin. The husband, much older than Tatiana. Even in death he seemed formidable and intimidating. If that was what the man had needed, Naum the little priest regretted not having taken his money; but he regretted even more not having heard his confession.

Tatiana had told him, "This money was to ensure your loyalty, to promise that you won't remember what you heard, and as a sacrifice to appease God's anger for all that he had done. Look at me," she said. "Look at me."

Naum said to Tatiana, "God knows the truth."

Beneath the presentation in the coffin Naum saw a deeper person residing. Was it a boy? Perhaps a little boy not unlike Naum himself. Perhaps if he could have found his childhood nakedness, the boy would have confessed. But so much money and ego stood in the space where a relationship might have taken root and grown, a confession would have been like watering a flower made of fine French silk.

Naki Q told Father, "One hundred cabs. One hundred drivers. One hundred black leather coats."

Solemn as a deacon on the day of his priestly ordination, one hundred drivers stood respectful and focused, silent sentinels stationed in the very back of the church, mute witnesses through the entire funeral service.

One hundred cabs, Naki?

Yes.

Naum was surprised.

Tatiana was not.

Outside, the son, Sergei, told the priest, "You didn't know? My father somehow came to own every cab medallion in this part of the city."

The undertaker's men lined them up.

The cabs.

The hearse.

The limo with mother and son.

Naum's old '66 Chevy.

He always drove his own car to the graveyard.

One hundred yellow taxi cabs in procession, with Q the Cop, in all his parody police regalia, halting traffic on the street outside the church and directing the procession from the parking lot, ebullient, beside-himself ecstatic, as each cab driver tipped his cap, saying, "Thank you, Officer."

———•———

AFTER URANIA'S FUNERAL, Father Naum had a new line. "Yes, I have seen a U-Haul truck in a funeral procession. But . . . it was empty."

Paper Crinkle

Just as the body has to be born when it has completed its time in the womb, so the soul has to leave the body when it has completed in the body the time assigned to it by God.

—St. Anthony the Great

A T THE CHURCH, when she was young, Isabelle was the only one loved by everyone. All the girls in our Teuta Ladies' Baking Society, even Philoxenia, who refused to join, even she loved Isabelle, and that's saying something.

"Love your church," Isabelle constantly reminded the kids in the church school.

She read the kids Bible stories and the lives of the saints. "You know Saint Nicholas lived by the sea. His parents were very rich."

She told her son, Timothy, and Katherine, her daughter, and Naum, who grew up to be our priest, and all the students in her fifth-grade class, "When Saint Nicholas's parents were gone . . ."

"Where'd they go, Mommy?" Katherine was the kind of kid who questioned everything.

Me? I never married, never had kids. I kept company with

my neighbor, Joey, but if I'd had kids, I don't think I could be so patient. Other parents or teachers? Betcha a box o' Dawn Doughnuts they'd likely as not have been annoyed by Katie's interruptions.

Not our Isabelle. "It means they went to heaven with God, Katie," she said.

"Means they died," Timmy said.

There was no getting nothing by the kid, Isabelle's Katie. Never missed a day of school. Never late, not once. Grades? Nothing below a B. And pretty too.

Isabelle did her daughter's hair and dressed her up every day for school like a perfect little dolly. Soon as she got a chance though, Katie the tomboy was outside after school in dungarees swinging from the trees and having fistfights, rolling in the dirt with Timmy and his friends. Girl could swing a broomstick halfies-bat too, knock those half-balls to the roof across Third Street.

Timmy loved to pull the long blond braids Isabelle put in his sister's hair. Isabelle thumped him on the head whenever she caught him, smoothed his cowlick, and told him, "Timmy, button your collar and straighten your tie."

Isabelle told her class, "Saint Nicholas gave away the better part of his parents' money to the poor and went to live with his uncle, a bishop. His name was Nicholas too. Young Nicholas became a monk, and later he was a bishop, just like his uncle. He took care of God's people. He never wrote books about our faith, but he lived and worked with the everyday people, and he loved our Lord Jesus, and His Mother, and the Church, and the saints who were before him, and he taught the people to love God and

God's Church, and that's why we remember Saint Nicholas and love him so much. He's one of us."

Timmy wanted to know if Saint Nicholas worked at the neighborhood putty factory. His mother told him, "No. And he didn't pull his sister's hair, either."

James, Isabelle's husband, was an ex-Navy man. He worked in the factory with the rest of the neighborhood men, but James worked in the office. He finished high school on the GI Bill and then did college accounting courses at night.

He used to say, "If you saw pictures of my Isabelle, from around the time we met, damn if she didn't look like Veronica Lake, maybe a little shorter, but prettier." Us Albanian girls tended toward the not-so-tall side.

Two-Beer Eddie said, "Yeah, James, and why she picked you is what we can't figure."

Isabelle would gather her class, measure each one. "Stand still, Naum."

The boy had a temper. Naum hated the costumes, especially having to wear the *fustenella*, the Albanian skirt.

Isabelle would tell him the same thing she told her own kids: "You know what happens when you get mad. You only got to get glad again."

She'd buy the material, custom sew the costumes from the home country, take weeks to teach and rehearse our traditional dances, and how she stuffed a dozen kids in that big old Buick of hers and drove them all the way across the city to the statewide downtown ethnic festival and actually got our neighborhood kids to perform?

Amazing Isabelle, what we women of the Teuta Ladies'

Baking Society called her.

Girl could cook too, learned from her mother. Same mother who taught her to love God and the Church, a mother like the mother before her, like most of us had, right back to the time when Saint Paul came to our village on the coast of what he called Illyria in his letter to the church at Rome.

Isabelle was the first woman in our church to finish high school. Big deal back then. She was the first to go to what they used to call business school, learned to type, take dictation, how to run an office.

The tiny two-story hospital where most of the neighborhood was born, the one run by the factory—well, some of us were born at home, but Isabelle ran the office at the hospital there on the factory grounds.

She knew what each of our fathers owed for our birth and the exact amount of cash they had to pay each week out of their pay envelope.

She teased that we were all so poor we had to be born on the installment plan, her kids too, and she told the kids that if they didn't behave, she'd have them repossessed.

And let me tell ya, we loved our kids. They practically got their faces kissed off every Sunday by all us old nunnas. Made us smile too, seeing the boys making faces and wiping off our kisses. Especially that Naum.

But that Katie, she was sunshine in our lives. Sunshine in a Sunday dress. Stood on her stool from the time she was three, covered in flour, singing with all the ladies, baking the holy bread. Stood on the same stool and sang her heart out with the choir too.

Katie, that's what we called our Katherine, Isabelle's daughter, came home from first year of high school in the vice principal's car all bandaged up with her braids cut off, her books in shreds, and her clothes in tatters.

"Couple o' jealous girls," the vice principal told Isabelle. She assured James and Isabelle it wouldn't happen again.

Senior girls caught Katie in the girls' room, beat her head against the porcelain sink, cut off her braids with razor knives, tore up her books and clothes, dunked her face in the toilet, and left her in the stall. That'll teach 'er book-smart ass. Katie put up a fight, but it was one too little against one too many.

All of us remember Katie's funeral. Isabelle found her in the morning, on the floor by her bed. The naïve cruelty that left Katie face down in the stall came like a wraith in the night and finished its work while she slept. More than one family in our neighborhood was never the same.

We could see the change in James and Isabelle, at church, at work. They didn't go out much; house over on Third Street always looked closed up. Hardly a light in the window. No decorations or tree at Christmastime. No more baking smells coming down Third Street. No more Buick full o' kids.

Timmy started acting out more and more. Got sent away to some military boarding school. Probably where he started doing drugs.

James got quiet, and Isabelle got grouchy. Who could blame 'em? But they never blamed God, and they never stopped coming to church.

Nobody mentioned it much after a while, even like asking, "How ya doing?" Even that woulda been cruel.

"Least people got that much sense," my friend Joey said.

Naum was our priest by the time that good-looking detective girl, K.C. King, called him.

Timmy was naked, lying between the door jamb and the bathroom door of his second-floor apartment, one arm stretched out over his head. Detective King told Naum, "It's called rigor mortis," when Naum asked why Timmy looked the way he did.

"How did you know to call me?" Naum wanted to know.

K.C. King handed Naum a handwritten prayer.

O Lord, grant me the strength to endure the fatigue of the coming day and all the events that take place during it.

K.C. said, "He wrote your name and cell on the back."

———•———

"HELLO, ISABELLE," Naum said. "James there?"

He listened while she called him to the phone. He could hear *Jeopardy* on the TV in the background. They were probably eating supper in front of the set.

"Father," James said. "Everything okay?"

Naum still felt funny when people who had probably changed his diaper kissed his hand or called him Father. He knew, as a person got older, any knock on the door, any phone call, was usually somebody wanting something or had some kind of disturbing news attached to it.

"James, Timmy could use a little help," Naum said. "You don't have to rush, but think you could meet me at his place, maybe an hour? That too soon?"

Isabelle was in the background asking, "What's wrong, James? What's the priest want?"

James told Naum, "We'll get ready and come over."

Detective King had the uniforms move the squad cars from out front. She waited upstairs in Timmy's apartment.

It upset Naum to see the police going through Timmy's place, him lying there, officers sifting every drawer, every closet, jacket pocket, cabinet, sofa cushion, cupboard top, under beds, and between the mattresses. He excused himself and went down the stairs.

Naum was out on the porch when they arrived. "James, Nunna."

She was nobody's fool. She knew. Naum could tell. "Where's my Timmy?" Her voice gave it away.

Naum tried to persuade her to wait. "Just for a minute, please, Nunna, while James and I go up to see him."

Isabelle was trying to push past when K.C. came down. She said, "Mr. and Mrs. Korca?" The detective led them up.

Naum followed. Before he reached the landing he could hear Isabelle, like her soul was leaving her body.

———•———

MEN AND WOMEN ARE NOT EQUAL, Naum always thought. Men have bigger muscles, bigger brains, bigger lung capacity, so they can serve the woman. Mankind, *anthropos*, is a woman. Just as the Virgin is an icon of the Church, and just as the Church conceives while remaining virginal and gives birth to new members in Christ, so all women bear that potential for conceiving and renewing life.

We are in them for nine months. "They are the gate of heaven," Naum would tell the boys. "Open the door for her. If there's only one seat, she gets it. She is your superior. You may live up to be her equal, but a different kind of equal, a complementary equal."

———◦—◦———

YEARS LATER, AFTER JAMES DIED, Naum went to visit Isabelle in the nursing home. She said to him, "Oh, are you working here too? I'm working here now."

"I came to visit you, Nunna," Naum said to his old Sunday school teacher.

She was in the cafeteria at a round table with several other women. She said, "I don't live here."

Naum said, "Okay, Nunna. I'm just happy to see you."

"They can't find out I'm pregnant," she whispered. "They'd want to fire me from my job if they found out."

Her hair was newly styled. Isabelle smelled good. She always insisted on being smartly dressed, on doing her own makeup. Even today, Naum noticed, she'd done quite a job, from her clean black slip-on penny loafers to her perfectly pressed blue slacks, her crisp white blouse, her red sweater and jewelry, maybe a little lipstick on her teeth, just a little.

Naum said, "How ya sleeping, Nunna?"

She said, "You know, I carried these children in me, and when God knows it's time, it's time."

Naum said, "God knows the truth."

"I went by Four-Twenty-Four last night," she said.

He knew it was their old address on Third Street.

"I looked in the window." She said, "Timmy and Katie were sitting on the couch watching *Jeopardy* with James. I left supper for them in the oven."

Naum knew the entire block of row houses had been razed. Now it was nothing more than an overgrown lot full of rubble.

She said, "And you know they've got a rotten priest at our church right now. If you love our church like I taught you, you should help them get a new one. This one's emptied out the church. Nobody was there when I went yesterday. The parking lot was empty. My Buick was the only car there. And it's not like a good birth, the way he gets them out. No. The whole place was empty because of him, in a bad way. Yelling at God's people because of paper crinkle."

The other women at the table were looking at him now. One of them said, "Are you a priest?"

Naum lowered his head.

Isabelle said, "Put out your hand."

He did.

She crumbled a handful of potato chips into his palm and held him with her eyes. She said, "They taste better crinkled."

An angry person is like a willful epileptic, who through an involuntary tendency breaks out in convulsion and falls down.
                                        —Saint John of the Ladder

It was a Sunday the year before James died that Naum heard the paper crinkling during Liturgy. It made him so angry he couldn't see to read the prayers. Unwrapping candy during the Gospel? Naum cut off the reading mid-chant, chastised the people with a look, went in, closed the Royal Doors and the curtain, no sermon, and was still so self-incensed by the time of

Communion he didn't want to commune—himself or anyone.

Some of the altar servers were afraid. Some thought he was a self-aggrandizing fool, a gold-plated *it's-all-about me* hypocrite.

Deacon Dionysios could see the shame and anger distorting the face of his friend. He put his hand on Naum's shoulder and got close in his ear. "We're not wrestling here against flesh and blood, Father. We got other things trying to rule us. Ya got evil things trying to creep through the cracks, even into the heavenly places."

The people venerated the cross in silence. They could tell Naum was steaming mad. They'd known him all his life. He was born at Isabelle's hospital.

Later Naum's wife, Greta—we all love her—she told him, "Poor Isabelle was crying for Katie and Timmy, sobbing to stop your heart. She's like a little girl now. James unwrapped the cellophane. He gave her a lozenge so she could catch her breath."

Naum, the priest, would have done anything if only he could have taken back his angry words and actions.

I was almost ninety when he confessed to me. "Louisa," Father Naum told me, "I wish my father would have missed a payment and Isabelle would have had me repossessed."

A quick movement of the millstone can grind in one moment and do away with more of the soul's grain and fruit than another crushes in a whole day. So we must understand and we must pay attention, for a strong sudden wind may fan a blaze that will cause more damage to the field of the heart than a lingering flame could ever manage to achieve.

—Saint John of the Ladder

The Tunnel

H<small>E WENT OUT THERE</small>, and lucky man, he found her, in her short tight outfit, tattoos and piercings, the jet black hair and Doc Marten combat boots. He couldn't believe it.

How many churches had her mother called? There were more than forty in the city. Forty-something Orthodox churches. *Services are as follows . . . Please leave a message.* Not one had answered or returned her call.

Then somehow Mom remembered, *Ah! The priest who baptized her. Wonder if he's still alive?* And before she left for her four-to-midnight shift in the ER, the trauma nurse took a chance and called Father Naum at Saint Alexander the Whirling Dervish Orthodox Church.

And damn if the dude didn't answer.

And damn if he didn't say, "Okay. I'll go and see what I can see."

They call it the tunnel, there in the perpetual shadows under the elevated train. The section that runs up above and shadows Kensington Avenue. Elevated train tracks two stories overhead that snake for almost thirteen miles through Philadelphia, from

Bridge and Pratt up north, diving underground for a while under the skyscrapers of downtown Philly, coming up for air, not bothering to look back at William Penn atop the City Hall tower, and heading out to 69th Street on the city's western edge.

They call the boys and girls who work under that Kensington Avenue stretch tunnel-boys or tunnel-girls. Selling themselves for eight to ten bags a night, in and out of cars, eight to ten times a night.

Ten dollars a pop. Cheapest. Purest. Most plentiful and potent forget-about-life poison a person in pain could ever pay the price to pump into their veins.

Out there in the open, hidden right in front of everybody's open eyes.

She was one of the most infamous, this little girl Father Naum had baptized. Maybe he'd been doing it too long, Naum. No matter how he tried, and despite her mother's reminders, he could not remember baptizing the girl standing in front of him in the tight net clothing with the blue-black lips. He couldn't believe he'd actually found her. Elisa. It just came to him, her name.

Encrusted. She looked like a Google map from space, street-grime delineating every avenue, pore, crevice, and crack on her fingers, forehead, arms, pretty face, and throat.

Bright blue eyes shining out, looking at the old priest as if to say, *Now, please don't take this personally.* Elisa, the street girl, took the chocolate milk Naum offered and bounced it off his head.

The corner of the carton left a dent, which either became permanent or had been there all along and he had just never noticed, till now. He couldn't remember which.

Nothing personal, dude. Just don't waste my time. Out here to make money, not to talk to religious do-goods. Only after the same thing every other goddamn guy in every other goddamn car coming down the goddamn avenue is after, after dark.

Same con. Different suit. *Dude—nothing personal.*

Once this avenue under the tunnel had been the center of immigrant life in the Kensington and Fishtown communities of Philadelphia.

As a boy Naum often accompanied his grandmother, Llamba, as she went with her wire cart on wheels to Honest John the greengrocer, to the butcher Mister Steinman, to Schmidt the baker, to the Yankee dairyman for cheese.

"You, be quiet," she told the boy Naum in the only language she knew. She'd been sixty years in America by the time it was all said and done and never learned to speak English.

Naum couldn't understand why one night a week his nunna sat, fascinated, in front of the old black-and-white 1958 Philco TV, watching Walter Brennan on *The Real McCoys*. How does she understand it?

"Whatcha watching, Nunna?" he'd ask in their language.

Grandmom Llamba shushed him and answered in the one word of English that made her happy. "Grandpappy."

Nunna's husband had died many years before. She'd been a widow living alone for longer than she'd been a bride.

Many of the women in our neighborhood worked near Howard and Oxford Streets in the local sweater factory workshop, assembling various parts of the product and being paid piecemeal, by the amount of work they produced. Llamba did too.

Once when young Naum went with his father to see the old woman, she was hiding in her kitchen crying behind a cupboard when a gunshot resonated through the house.

Naum's father shoved his son to the floor. "Mom," he called in Albanian, "what did you do?"

From her hiding place she told him she'd been cleaning and found her dead husband's pistol and a dusty box of little bombs. She'd thrown the box of little bombs into the wood-burning pot-belly stove in the kitchen, and now the bullets were exploding, piercing the stove and ricocheting around the kitchen.

"Was the box full?" Naum's father asked old Nunna.

All she could do was sob.

On the avenue under the El, with her shopping cart and her young grandson Naum in tow, Llamba wanted eggs. Little boy Naum knew better than to speak after she'd admonished him to silence with a finger-thump on the head. Even in his frustration he was afraid to speak as she stood there in her black widow's garb, going back and forth with Samuel Barenbaum, the Jewish grocer who worked with Honest John.

"Kid." Mister Barenbaum appealed to Naum.

Llamba thumped her grandson on the head, this time with her cane. *"Nuk flas."* Don't speak.

"Lady," the man in the white apron said, "how am I supposed to help you, for crying out loud?"

She took a potato from the bin, bent forward, the potato in perfect position to be laid, and made the noise, "Buck buck buck buck," like a chicken.

"Oh!" said Sam the grocer. "You want eggs."

It was late now. Naum was on the avenue again, under the tunnel. But the years had swept away the old immigrant communities from Kensington and Fishtown, swept away the black-garbed widows with their wire wheeled carts, Samuel Barenbaum the greengrocer, Mister Steinman the butcher, Schmidt the baker, the barbers and the dairymen who sold the cheese, even Shooky's, the bar on the corner—they were no more to be found in the working-class area that used to be known as the Workshop of the World.

A new community of arrivals had taken their turn at bat—Vietnamese, Indonesian, Korean, Cambodian, Jamaican, Hispanic—a colorful collage of hardworking people, all swinging for the fences, running the bases, trying to get their kids out of Kensington alive, hoping not to strike out along the way.

Before he'd found Elisa, standing with his hands in the air, Naum told the man camouflaged in shadows, "This doesn't have to be a robbery. I prefer to give you whatever you want."

The man attempting to rob him told Naum, "Try being quiet."

Naum made a wordless prayer asking Llamba to ask God to protect him and the man.

The man took a long look at Naum. "You a reverend?"

"I am."

"Why ya 'round here, Rev?"

"I was born in Kensington Hospital," Naum answered.

"You was born in a rehab?" The man was almost amused.

"It wasn't a rehab back then."

He perused Naum and said, "Yeah, well, you are pretty old."

"I'm looking for a girl I baptized. Elisa. Her mom's worried. I wonder if she's out here." Naum offered the man a chocolate milk. He'd been told people using certain street drugs often craved sweets.

"She usually hang out up around Kensington and Somerset."

The man took the chocolate milk. He said, "I don't know why you wanna bother. I mean, we're already so far busted out, it ain't likely we coming back."

The El rolling overhead rattled the beams and shook the pavement. Naum looked up.

When he looked again, the man was gone, as if he'd been sucked down the tunnel in the wake of the train.

Naum felt shaky, but there was no one to hold on to.

Thanks to the man who wanted to rob him, Naum found Elisa, and after Elisa bounced the chocolate milk off Father's head, they sat down together on the grime-encrusted slab and stared at each other. Naum took off his skufia while he rubbed his head and tried to get into hers.

They sat on the steps of a Methodist church up near Somerset, and Elisa said to him, "Everybody out here already knows there's only so many versions of the same twisted man. You see him in every vacant lot and doorway, every town and city. Just blink and there he is, out here on the hunt. Offering you a ride around the corner, same seat Mommy sits in. Ain't that great?" she told Naum.

What else could Naum do but listen? All he had was listening. Even with baptism as a start, there had to be more to build the bridge. First, try to understand. The Fathers say you can listen another's soul into existence.

Elisa said, "And wouldn't that lady's husband, her kids' daddy, wouldn't that man be proud if only Mommy and the kids could see his sorry ass now, out here, with me? All varieties and flavors, you just name your game. Can't blame the normal world. They look at it and don't even see it. Sit in the same damn seat Daddy got me sitting in and don't even smell it, they hearing the same damn music, digging the beat, but no-wise get the lyrics."

———

THERE WAS AN ORTHODOX BROTHERHOOD clergy meeting scheduled later that morning at Naum's parish. He put on the white apron and prepared the breakfast, happy it wasn't a fasting day. Bacon, eggs, coffee, and toast, in from under the tunnel, smelled so good. Naum's second favorite line in the Gospel was the Master telling the disciples, "Come, have breakfast."

Elisa set out the places and poured juice in each glass. The girl with her bottom peeking out of her too-tight outfit asked for two aprons. She covered herself, front and back, bottom and top. And even stayed after to help Father Naum with the cleanup.

None of the clergy offered to help. They were polite to Elisa, but no more so than they would've been to any waitress or bus person in any café.

Naum thought perhaps one might've asked, during the meeting, "Who is that girl?" He would like to have told them, if he could, about what he'd experienced out there under the tunnel the night before, about the complex human geography of simple everyday life out there dying in the dark.

"You mother's shift at the ER starts at four, sweetie," Father Naum told Elisa. "Doris Drobish and the ladies are coming in any time now. Her and some of the ladies are sewing sweaters, like your grandmom and my grandmom used to do, except now it's to give to single moms at the shelter."

Elisa was on her seventh cup of coffee.

"Our grandmothers had hard choices, Elisa. I remember your

grandmother. Her name was Martha. She dressed in black, just like my grandmother. She was a young widow. I'm pretty sure your grandfather got killed loading coal where he worked over at the railroad."

Naum said, "They were tough women. Strong. Resolute. Creative too. She raised your mom and your Uncle Billy by herself. Couldn't've been easy. Kids gave her a hard time. Probably like I did my parents."

"This decaf?" Elisa asked.

"Always been something out here trying to make you forget who you really are, your true self. Where you're really from. And where you're really going, ya know, ultimately, I mean. I think we forget all that. Maybe we've been distracted by how much stuff we have, the stuff that becomes stuff we have to deal with."

"How much we have." She almost laughed but stopped herself out of pity for the priest.

"Truthfully, Elisa, I don't know the answer. But somehow or another they managed to stay connected to God and the Church, that older generation of women, and not end up being fooled when people promised something better somewhere out there. Never got caught up in that tunnel vision. They remembered who they were."

He wasn't sure Elisa understood, but he knew he had to find a kind, non-accusatory way to plant the seed of her deeper remembering. He wished he knew the name the Lord Jesus called her by, the one on the white stone.

But then again, he couldn't even remember baptizing the kid. Felt like a failure as a priest, as a father in the Gospel, not to mention as a person.

Elisa said to him, "I remember my baptism."

Naum was stunned as she described the day in detail. She laid it out, right there in front of him. It made him ashamed.

Then she said, "I don't knit or sew, with yarn or thread, but maybe I'm creative, like them. I knit my thoughts together on paper. I have a rule, from when I was little. Every day I write *something*. Something about the people who come in and out of my life and about the things that happen. Someday I'm gonna sew them all together in a book. And Father, I do remember who I am, and where I'm from, and I do know what you mean by that. You're not talking about the old neighborhood or the old country, things like that that fade away. That's not where we're going, ultimately. It's just sometimes I forget, or maybe you're right, maybe it is too much stuff, stuff around us makes it hard to keep it in mind."

Naum said, "Me too." Then he said, "And I'd read your book, if you'd let me."

Elisa said, "I wrote something for you, but only you can read it, okay?"

He said, "Understood."

"I'm tired, Father."

He said, "You wanna take a nap in the back, you could. You'd be safe here. There's cushions on that bench in the back."

"Near the icon of the blind lady?"

"Yes, Saint Matrona of Moscow. And after I'll drive you up to see your mom. She's worried, kid."

"She's only worried about herself." Elisa was not impressed. Or maybe Elisa really was just tired. "She's self-obsessed," Elisa said. "All my life she's either ignored me for the men she was with, got me and her high, or bought me off."

It wasn't angry or resentful, the way Elisa said it. It was just matter-of-fact, like saying her name was Elisa.

Elisa handed Father Naum a folded paper. "Here," she told him. "This is what I wrote. I wrote it for you while you were hob-nobbing with your fellow wizards."

Wizards. Made Naum smile.

Elisa said, "And damn, Padre, they were some fat-ass boys, weren't they? Most of your meeting all they talked about was what they could or couldn't eat during *Kreshme*."

"You think?" Naum was surprised she remembered their name for Great Lent.

When she started to describe one or two of the clergy from various synagogues and churches, clergy she knew from the tunnel—*pathetic*, she called them—that's when Naum heard Doris and the Teuta Ladies' Baking Society coming in the door.

Street-savvy Elisa changed the subject. "They can put away the bacon, can't they?"

The ladies saw and sewed and whispered.

If Elisa had any regard for them, any embarrassment or anger about her situation, she didn't show it. She passed out on the bench.

Father Naum asked Madeline to come in and cover Elisa.

He went into the temple, lit the censer, and stood before the icon of the Theotokos and Child.

He read her note.

He made the cross.

And had he not been so exhausted, he probably would've wept, for Llamba and for Mister Barenbaum, for Grandpappy, and for the man who tried to rob him, for the Vietnamese and the

Cambodians, for chocolate milk, and for his father and the little bombs, for Shooky's Taproom on the corner, for the barbers and the bakers, the butcher and the man who sold the cheese, for everything that was caught up and swept away down the tunnel. Would have stood and wept for a long time, for Elisa and her mother, for himself, would have wept then and there.

REMEMBER ME O LORD

A cold stone step
On this bleak avenue
Where no one
Wants to sit
A shadowed doorway
Along this street
Where no one
Wants to sleep
An abandoned shell
In this crumbling neighborhood
People no longer call a home
A darkened car
With someone inside
Who no one wants to touch
But I am sitting here, Lord
I am sleeping here
I am being touched
And I am dying of this darkness
Lord, please send someone
Who will remember my name
I am here, Lord, and I am Yours

Rabbi's Question

I will enter Thy House, I will worship toward Thy Holy Temple in fear of Thee.

FATHER NAUM ENTERED THE CHURCH. It was early. Very early. The temple was lovely, cold, and quiet.

The woodwork was steeped in spice and smoke, like barrel wood aged in frankincense. The fragrance of life was ingrained in every fibrous layer—year come and year gone, each petition, every promise, every prayer permeated the whorls of every balustrade, panel, and rail.

He greeted the icons. He struck a match. He lit his candle. He placed it in the box of sand. A thousand who had gone before in the Faith were illuminated. Their love for Christ was animated in Naum by Christ's love for them.

I stand before the gates of Thy temple and yet I refrain not from my evil thoughts.

With a shiver he fought off his fear. Vlad was a wicked man. Vlad was a violent man. Naum had his own struggle with wickedness. His own violence. Sensing his paralysis in time, he told himself, "When is there not work in the Garden?" He said to his fear, *Kairos tou poiesai to Kyrio.*

"It is time for the Lord to act," Naum whispered as he stood before the Royal Gate. "For Your law has been broken."

———•———

HE LIKED TO TAKE HIS TIME on Sunday morning. It was a one-day-a-week luxury. He liked to pray the entrance prayers slowly. To say the Jesus Prayer with every candle lit. To savor every moment of his quiet time alone amidst the great cloud of witnesses with God. Was it possible, he thought, to be alone with God?

The steam in the pipes began to rattle, and the radiators hissed as he entered the altar and made the prayers and lesser metania, bowing before the throne.

Naum remembered the old woman. Vlad and the old woman, Maureen. Her husband was the rabbi at the temple across the avenue. What a lovely man, the rabbi. What a fine woman, his wife.

"Naum," Rabbi would say, "tea is the thing for us now that we're getting older. We sit and discuss everything from garments animals may wear on the Sabbath to the correct way to eat a scallion. And what do we find?"

"We find, my friend," Naum said, "that we see and relate to our Creator and to the world in much the same way. But that we need glasses now to see the book."

"And our beards," said Rabbi, looking over his steel-framed glasses. "I think they're virtually the same, so why does mine look longer, good Father?"

"Your knitted vest?" Naum said.

"Could be," Rabbi said, "but I think it's because I'm shorter."

"Or because my cassock makes me look taller?"

"Could be, my Orthodox colleague, but beards aside, the reason we have a similar vision, what makes sense most, for me, is your penchant for saying what is *not*. What *God* is not. This," and he held up a finger, "this is our GCF—our *greatest common factor*—your apophatic approach. Of course, there are differences," Rabbi said. "One in particular. So I'm asking you, confidentially, as a man and a friend, not as the sage theologian you think yourself to be, but as the mensch I know you to be." For a man of seventy-five, Rabbi had not lost that effervescent curiosity that kept his mind spinning like a three-ring gyroscope laser dreidel. "*Is* he the one?"

Naum wondered how others might answer. How do you answer a man, a long-tenured professor, with honor upon honor, with a university library, no less, named after him? Why would so authentic a man ask such a question, and of Naum? A rabbi, no less, fluent in Hebrew, Aramaic, Yiddish, French, and Russian, and so fluent in these, and in German, that he quoted riddles and made jokes in these other tongues. He was well read in Latin, "and even a little Albanian and Greek, I have." Rabbi smiled. "But who on the factory floor would notice?"

A little? The Greeks in the neighborhood thought he was a villager from Epirus, and the Albanians claimed him too.

As a young man, Rabbi Aaron Strauss was dropped behind enemy lines during the war as part of an American tactical unit doing reconnaissance in the Balkans. He was wounded, rescued by partisans, and convalesced, hidden in the home of the local Orthodox priest.

At home the priest and his family spoke Albanian. At church and in public, they spoke Greek. The family of the priest nursed Rabbi, made sure he had kosher food, prayer books, and everything he needed.

Rabbi Aaron used to say, "If I wore a kilt, the fustenella, it would be Albanian. They have style. And were I a Christian, Greek it'd be for me."

Maureen, Rabbi's wife, was brokenhearted when their forty-year-old daughter, Carol, died not long after giving birth to twins.

"It's too late in life to be having children," Maureen thought, but she would never say anything to her daughter. How could she presume to tell her daughter, Carol, the doctor?

Rabbi, on the other hand? His wife Maureen told him every day the entire time of Carol's pregnancy. "She's too old, Aaron."

Carol was a doctor, and she married a doctor, Samuel Weiss. After Carol's death, Doctor Samuel Weiss had no talent, he told Rabbi, for raising twins.

Seventy-year-old Maureen and seventy-five-year-old Rabbi Aaron Strauss were now the main providers for two-year-old Seth and his sister Sarai. Doctor Weiss and his new wife, his practice manager, Kathy, came to visit from San Francisco at least twice a year, "weather and surgeries permitting." Rabbi smiled. "But the trust fund is there. And money? If you have money, you are wise and good-looking and can sing well, too."

Naum wondered why, after all these years of friendship—over twenty years—why now? The question—the anointed one, David's heir—why was Rabbi asking now?

Everyone knew, Naum had confessed it freely many times. "If

I weren't Orthodox, I would not be a Western Christian. I'd be an Orthodox Jew."

Even if others didn't, Rabbi and Naum both knew the reason. But now was not the time to say it again. Brokenhearted Naum knew, the Hebrew Bible said, for everything, there is a season.

———•———

MORE THAN HIS DAUGHTER CAROL'S DEATH and struggling to raise the twins, it was the fact that one of Naum's flock had beaten and robbed Rabbi's wife, Maureen, now seventy years old. A previously self-sufficient woman who loved going daily to the market, meeting friends, gossiping, cleaning house, always at the synagogue, relaxing in the evening, watching TV with her husband, ambulatory and healthy, revivified by the presence of her grandchildren, made young by caring for her Carol's twins. Why had Vlad, the Orthodox boy, why had he ended all that?

Naum had been in the courtroom. He was there for the trial. He saw the photo exhibits. An old woman beaten black and blue. He heard the evidence. Broken bones. Fractured skull. Unimaginable pain. He sat with Vlad's mother, Alyona. She cried the whole time. The judge asked the priest, Naum, "Would you like to address the court?"

"No," Naum said, "I am here only to support Alyona, and the Rabbi, and his wife Maureen."

Between sobbing Alyona would whisper, "It's my fault. It's my fault." Alyona had been a single mother since coming to America.

Her husband, Dimitre, had rank and status at home. He was obdurate in his ways. He refused to learn English. "Starting all over again is something women can do because they have little character or pride," he said. "Let them humble themselves. But for Dimitre, trading my dignity for American pie? No."

He abandoned her and Vlad and went back. She finished school, put in her hours, and was certified as a CDAC, a Certified Drug and Alcohol Counselor, and was hired in a Veterans Hospital rehab.

The rehab needed a driver. Alyona was able to get Vlad a job driving vets to appointments. "That's where I developed my habit," Vlad told the judge.

No one mentioned Vlad's girlfriend, Jennifer, frail and frightened, sitting in the last row. Vlad told her, "Either you go on the corner under the tunnel to earn our money"—they were both badly addicted—"or I beat the old Jew's wife when she goes to the market. And it will be your fault."

It was Jennifer, his girl, who turned him in.

Alyona had the appearance of a schoolgirl. It was common for people to think the slight woman with the pretty young face and the happy, open complexion was Vlad's older sister.

Vlad was nothing like his mother. Big and brooding, thick and temperamental, quick to judge and take action, no one ever doubted the young man with the big hands and powerful arms was the son of Dimitre.

———·———

IN PRISON VLAD WAS PLACED in a heroin detox unit. After the two-week mandatory blackout period, Naum went to see him. The CO, the guard, had Naum place his belongings, wallet, ID, keys, belt, and money in a locker. "Go into that room and wait," the corrections officer told Naum.

The CO came in and started with, "Take off your shoes." By the time he'd been fully strip-searched, Naum was having trouble catching his breath.

He dressed and went, carrying his shoes, through a second metal detector to a room with mesh wire benches bolted to the floor. An older woman with watery blue eyes asked as he was tying his laces, "Are you a priest?"

"Yes," said Naum.

"I come to see my son, Father, every week and put money in his commissary account. Money from my late husband's pension," she said. "He's been in and out of prison, my son, for thirty years. Maybe more."

Naum leaned in to hear, thinking she would like to keep her private business private.

She said, "Father." She started to tear up.

Naum took her hand.

"Last week I told him, son, I've been to the doctors. I have only three months to live," she said.

"God have mercy," Naum said.

"You know what he said to me, Father?" Her voice was becoming flat and more distant.

"I can't imagine," Naum said.

"He said, 'I guess this means I ain't getting any more f——money in my commissary account.'"

Naum couldn't think what to say. He said, "How old is your son?"

"Fifty-six," she told Naum.

Father Naum wanted to ask her, "Lady, what are you doing here?" He wanted to tell her, "Go out in the sunshine and live your last three months. Prepare your soul. Give time to God." But instead he sat, holding her hand, looking at the vacuum in this mother's eyes. He said, "You go to church. I can tell. You've done your best to be a good mother. The seeds you have planted in your son's heart may grow after you're gone. Only God knows. You've done your part. The rest is in God's hands. You can do whatever you have to do now, in peace."

The CO called Naum through to the room where Vlad was waiting. It seemed to Naum that Vlad had gotten even bigger. His orange jumpsuit was so tight and small it appeared to Naum as if Vlad had donned the prison garb and wore it in purposeful disdain, mocking the system, telling them by his physical rupture of the penitentiary attire that "not even your stupid uniform can contain me."

"Face forward. No touching," the CO commanded before chaining Vlad to a metal ring embedded in the floor.

Naum took out the prayer book and icon approved by the prison chaplain. Vlad laughed. Turning his head, he said to Naum, "Keep it. I can live without your Jesus," and spun it sideways, hitting Naum in the face. "Useless dreck. What does any of it mean anyway? You're mentally ill. You and your imaginary God."

Now the guard came over, looked at Naum, and said, "Enough?"

Vlad stood to be unlocked. "Don't come again," he told Naum. "You and your God are off my list, permanently."

———•———

NAUM KNEW it would be a long eight years. For Alyona. For Rabbi and Maureen, and for Vlad. But this Sunday morning, preparing the proskomedia alone just before Liturgy, time for Naum had ceased to be linear, sequential, unrepeatable, irreversible, a paralysis. Time was a chalice of eternity. Time was now.

"Rabbi," Naum had asked, "you've taken care of the congregation for so long. Have you ever had one family, that one difficult family?"

"Me? No." Rabbi loved to tease. Then he said, "You try. You try. You cajole. You appeal. You plead. You try sugar. You act as if you're the law. Nothing. So"—he held up his hands in surrender—"to hell with them." His smile was not one of triumph. "Take care of the others who accept, who do not shame God or themselves—or shame you, for that matter, or the congregation of faith. Is God and faith somehow diminished by one person who bears His name in vain? The one who refuses to bow down to God or to anyone, who thinks God needs our bowing down, who doesn't realize it's not for God that we bow, it's for us, to learn our place in the universe . . . that there are things greater than we? And that one person, well, you know, for now, anyway. God knows the truth and perhaps will save that one, or us even, in time."

Naum said, "Yes. He saves in ways which are known to Him alone."

"*Mazel tov.*" Rabbi wished Naum health, and they took their tea together.

"I've been thinking about your question, Rabbi," Naum said. "From you, Israel, God has given Moses and the prophets. Our Master is a Jew. His Mother is a Jew. Aren't we the wild olive shoot grafted in? Your prayer, Rabbi, He no doubt hears. The One who walked with Adam in the Garden still invites us to eat with Him."

UNTIL HE STOOD UP FROM THE PEW, the man with the piercings, the shaved tattooed head, and the small pointed beard didn't look any larger than a small mountain. Naum's fear stood with him. Alyona stood with her son. They both came toward the deacon's door, where Naum waited. Alyona said nothing.

Vlad surveyed Naum, grinding the chain of his mother's restraint through his teeth. He said to Naum, "Keeping busy?"

Naum spoke to his fear. *When does evil let us rest?*

Before entering the altar, Naum bowed to the protopsaltis at the chanters' stand and said, "It is time for the Lord to act."

In the altar, diagonally across the apse above his head, the thick rope of the bellpull cut a swath across the rounded space. Naum grasped the rough braid hand over hand and bent his back to the prayer of the bell. With every pull, scattered time was gathered, its fragmentation healing.

The resonating truth of being rang out and time itself was resurrected, time was restored to its true calling as the chalice of God's love for His creation, and with each pull of the rope, creation moved toward God, and in the mystery of the never-ending Day of His Kingdom, God embraced His creation.

Alyona made the cross and stood through the Liturgy. Her son did not. Vlad followed Dimitre. We never saw him again.

Three-Stitch Prayer

———•———

T HEY WERE SITTING IN THE ER, Father Naum and the baby-faced matushka. Father Naum was holding a maroon-colored cloth banquet napkin, an oversized linen napkin, the kind you could've used as a bib, or a cover-up sarong, or a parachute if you needed to. It was soaked in blood. He was pressing down hard on the little boy's head. "Ya doing all right, kid?" old Naum asked him.

He wasn't crying as much as before, the kid. He said, "Is it gonna hurt?"

His name was Raphael. Father Naum called him Ralphie. "Yep, Ralphie, it's gonna hurt, but only like that girl Margie you told me about in the schoolyard pinching you 'cause you wouldn't let her kiss you. Won't hurt worse than that."

"That hurt," he said.

"Yeah, but you can take it. Right?"

"I guess so," Ralphie said.

His mother, Matushka Coleen, was the kind of kid you'd say was too pretty to be the wife of a priest. Somewhere in the middle, her hair color, between blonde and brown, straighter than a galvanized finishing nail. The girl couldn't have curled her hair with a heating coil off the space shuttle.

If she looked you in the eye too long, her crossed green eyes made you want to squeeze your eyelids shut. Coleen was tall and thin and rugged as a tin roof on a farm shed. Smarter in every department than her husband, the archpriest, Father James. Sharper than all the priests in our city Brotherhood, is what Naum said.

Matushka Coleen said, "He's a bastard."

"Me?" Ralphie said.

She didn't think he heard her. Coleen said, "No, sweetie, not you. Whoever didn't dry that floor you slipped on." Then she said "James" to Father Naum, so Ralphie couldn't hear.

Ralphie said, "How ya know it was a man?"

Kid had a point. His mother said, "Did I say it was a man? I said *whoever*."

Ralphie stuck his head up from the chair. "Then why did you say *he's* a—"

"Raphael." She cut him off. Mothers and first names. And that was that.

The doctor had an accent Naum couldn't peg. She was petite and dark, and if you were looking for that brisk, rehearsed, clinic-speak personal bedside manner that made you feel like the latest med-school techno-robotic patient with a state-of-the-art pulsar beating heart, dilating eyes, and realistic lifelike wounds, a digitally programmed specimen who breathes and has an almost true-to-life arrhythmic pulse—all the vital signs a doctor could ever want, *plus* an arm capable of receiving multiple simultaneous sterile IVs . . .

The one with the cold hands you just had to have checking your vitals, talking to you in med-tech, exhibiting all the symptoms and sympathy of an assembly-line factory worker under time-efficient preceptor pressure, ignoring you the whole time she was poking electronic records into her iPad . . . then this doctor was your girl.

People said, *There are priests just like her, Naum.*

Ralphie cursed a lot when she was putting in the stitches and surprised the whole clinic with some original names for the doctor when she stuck him with the needle.

The doctor asked what he was saying. Ralphie had employed some genuine colloquial one-of-a-kind neighborhood epithets Father Naum hadn't heard since Two-Beer Eddie stepped barefoot on a nail while building a menu stand for our parish Hot Dog Sunday.

Matushka told the doctor Ralphie was speaking our language and hoped she hadn't had language studies as a minor. Later Matushka told Father Naum, "He hears all that from his father."

Naum had been coming through the buzz of the banquet hall, winding his way through a crowd of five hundred, headed toward his assigned table when Ralphie slipped and whacked his head on the claw foot of a sixty-inch round, wobbly table seating ten.

The bishops were arrayed along a skirted table high up on a dais decorated with double-headed eagles. They were being served by a cadre of waiters in white shirts, bow ties, and long black aprons.

An oversized podium with an icon of Saint George stood center stage. All sorts of clerical headdress—*kamilavkas* and *klobuks*, plain black and jeweled, and the bishops' stovepipe hats—crowned every pontifical head. Father Naum swore their episcopal beards got longer every time they donned that imperial Byzantine headgear. Keeping up with imperial Byzantium was what was wearing Orthodoxy down, is what Naum said. Plywood painted gold?

The metropolitan, white topper with the silver cross on the front, stationed mid-table, struggled to eat his cold chilly-dilly cucumber soup without spilling it on his purple *riassa*.

The breeze from the overhead ceiling fans billowed the skirts of the head table and had all the wide-sleeved robes, the riassas, and the thin black monastic veils in full sail. Made Naum want to go fly a kite.

He was thinking to himself, *If we added up the value of all the jeweled chains, crosses, and ivory icon amulets on the dais . . .* It was right then that Ralphie did his thing. Two steps too slow, there was nothing Matushka Coleen, good catch that she was, could've done to save her boy. Ralphie went down like a novice skater on a frozen lake.

Father James wasn't what you'd call happy when Naum brought him to the scene. Who would've been? But hey, it's your kid, right? Maybe it's different in the neighborhood, who knows?

Naum? He would've told the bishop, "Vladika, that talk I was slated to give on prayer? Gotta cancel."

Father James had a spot others would've chewed incense to get. Keynote speaker at the Sobor? At the lavish banquet topping the week-long ecclesiastical Diocesan Assembly and Synodal Council? In front of twelve bishops?

Naum looked at James like, "What?"

Father James said, "What a thing. What a position to be in."

It was at that point that Naum took one of the maroon banquet napkins from the nearest table and dumped ice from one of the silver buckets into it. "Here, Matushka, press it on his head."

She turned and looked at her husband.

Naum applied the ice himself and mouthed the words "Gonna need a stitch" over Ralphie's head.

Ralphie was doing the boxer-wobble and saying, "It don't hurt."

Father James looked at Naum and said, "I won't forget this. What's your name?" Naum never wore the priestly pectoral cross, so Father James took a shot. "Subdeacon?"

"Yes, Father, bless." Naum took the priestly blessing.

"Thank you." Then James said to his Coleen, "He'll be okay, just find me after." He took an old skufia, the black skullcap Coleen had made, from his cassock pocket, dusted it off, and pulled at a thread. He said, "Weren't you supposed to make me a new one for tonight?"

At the ER she told Naum, "You don't get to be seminary dean by putting family first, you know."

"Dean?" Naum said.

"There's an opening. He wants it. And I'm sitting here with a stranger and a bleeding kid." Then she started to cry. But she wasn't sad. Coleen was angry, maybe more frustrated than angry. "I'm sorry," she said. "I don't even know your name, and we've been sitting here in this waiting room over an hour."

"I'm Naum."

"Are you a priest?"

"There's only one priest," Naum said.

They shook hands. Naum thought Coleen had hands you could

count on if you needed help. After it was all done, the unit secretary in the ER processed Coleen's payment information, then Coleen said to Naum, "Now what? I'm not going back there."

"You like ice cream, Ralphie?" Naum had asked Matushka, "Is it okay if I ask him?" He asked her permission first. Never a bad idea with mothers nowadays, any time, for that matter.

They sat in a booth in an old-fashioned ice cream parlor down the block. A milkshake for Matushka, black and white. Ralphie got a sundae. Banana split for Naum.

"What was he gonna talk about?" Naum asked.

"Who?" Matushka said, though she knew.

"Your husband."

Coleen said, "Wanna hear?"

"Yes."

"Good." Then she leaned over. "And I hope the bastard does okay without his text." She unfolded a typed sheet of notes.

Naum had to smile.

"You feeling okay, honey?" she said to Ralphie.

Ralphie touched the sore spot on his head and said, "It's stiff." He asked his mother, "Why'd she cut my hair?"

"You have three stitches," she said. "The doctor had to make a clean spot so she could see, and so we can keep it clean."

"It don't hurt," he said, and tapped his head.

"Novocaine?" Naum asked.

"Wait'll it wears off," Coleen said. "Whatever it is."

"Can he sleep?"

"Nurse told me there is no benefit to keeping him awake, even if it is a concussion. No longer recommended. In fact, she said, he needs to sleep to recover."

The waitress brought a kid's placemat and crayons, and Ralphie got to work.

Naum said, "I'd like to hear the talk, if you're up for it."

Coleen told Naum, "I'm the one who was a believer. Since I was a little girl, the family weirdo, that's me. A throwback to the Garden of Eden, my mother used to call me. When we met, I think James took an interest in the Church just to get me to pay attention to him."

"So God maybe saved him through you."

"Well, He's taking his time about it." Coleen smiled.

"He'll get there," Naum said. "Mankind is a woman."

Matushka Coleen knew Naum was talking about the Theotokos.

Naum said, "My Irish grandmother had eighteen kids. We called her Nanny. She used to say, 'God is slow but sure.'"

"God bless that woman. I suppose she knew. As for my guy? Slow ain't the word. The outside's getting there, but about half of James's interior's still under construction. We got a ways to go."

"Hard to be patient with the people closest to you, right?" Naum said.

"Yeah, easier with strangers. You don't have to live with them."

"Nobody knows the priest like his wife."

"God knows the truth," Matushka agreed.

"So, I get to hear the keynote," Naum said, "*and* a banana split? Unhappy I'm not."

Coleen said, "Starts with a quote from Metropolitan Anthony Bloom: 'You remember how you were taught to write when you were small. Your mother put a pencil in your hand, took your hand in hers, and began to move it.'"

"Good start," Naum said.

Matty Coleen said, "The rest, I wrote for him. Well, most of it."

Naum was surprised, but not really. He said, "Okay."

"If you don't want to hear, I understand. It's been a long night, and you missed your dinner. Chicken or fish? Because of us. I am so sorry."

"I prefer banana splits anytime," he said. "And I am interested to hear."

"There are three simple things." She said, "Probably not theological, you know, I mean, exactly correct. But they're my experience."

Maybe it was her crossed green eyes, or her little-girl, spaghetti-straight hair, or the strength in her bearing, or the obvious acuity and reasoning present in her judgment and the quality of her voice. "I feel like life is one big prayer," she said.

Maybe it was her heart. He felt it in the way she related to everyone—from the waiters, to the doctor, to the ER clerk, to Naum the ice cream-eating stranger across the table, or in her refusal to give up on loving a husband, preoccupied and missing his life going by as he was. Or maybe it was the light that came on in her eyes every time she looked at her little Ralphie. "Stop picking at your stitches, ya nudge."

Whatever it was, Naum was figuring this woman would've made a great priest, and he told her so. He said, "You were born to liturgize. You shoulda been the priest."

She told him, "I look that dumb to you?"

Judging by the little he knew of her, the girl was too savvy by a stretch, too comfortable in her own sexuality to be tempted outside the Trinitarian call, in the image of God, male and female He created them to be fruitful and multiply.

Here was a girl, Naum was sure, who saw, who sensed deep calling to deep, the seminal movement interwoven in the living movement of the Divine Liturgy. It's a harmonious iconicity in the liturgy of life, in the way a man and a woman are blessed by God in the community of marriage to participate in His creative, life-giving calling for them, calling each one of us into becoming, into being, into the life of the world to come.

When she got tired of him calling her Matushka, she asked Naum, "Think they got rank and title in heaven?"

Like many mothers of the Faith before her, Coleen seemed to carry a prenatal memory of the liturgical nature of our first home, in the Church of Paradise. Pheromone incense was all Naum could think to call that implicit recollection.

"You sing the psalms when you're doing housework?" she asked Naum.

"I pray the prayer when I'm scrubbing the bathrooms, 'cept the toilet," he said.

She was a natural theologian. She knew God by virtue of her being and by virtue of her ignorance of formal theology. The girl was comfortable being the bride and all that it entailed, because she believed in her flesh and in the deepest part of her being, that the Bridegroom loved her. This was one woman who saw no diminution in the obedience of her ordination in the eucharistic community as a daughter of the Theotokos.

"You are a priest, aren't you?" she said. "Want me to make you a new cassock?" She could tell he'd never noticed, till she mentioned it, just how frayed things had become.

When he didn't answer, she said, "Wore that on the ark, didn't ya, Noah?"

No whisper of the snake could deter Coleen from our common anamnesis—from her memory of the future, the call of our liturgical being. "I know where I'm from, who I am, and where I'm going," she said.

It was obvious to Naum, Coleen had eyes in her heart. He knew enough to listen and learn when he encountered a natural-born instrument of the Liturgy.

"Let me ask you," Coleen said, "when you go to pray, what's the first thing you ask for?"

Luckily she didn't leave Naum time to show what a novice he felt himself when it came to prayer.

"Prayer," she said. "You remember what Saint Paul wrote to the Church at Rome. 'Likewise the Spirit helps us in our weakness. For we do not know what to pray for as we ought, but the Spirit Himself intercedes for us with groanings too deep for words.'"

The seventh priestly prayer of Orthros reflected what Saint Paul had imparted to the community of believers at Rome.

God and Father of our Lord Jesus Christ . . .
Teach us your statutes, because we do not know how to pray as
we ought, unless You, Lord, guide us by Your Holy Spirit.

"On my own," Matushka Coleen said, "I don't even have faith. He is the author and the finisher of our faith. And I sure don't have a prayer on my own. So the first thing I ask for when I go to pray is prayer."

Naum wanted to ask about the second thing, but he'd gotten to the place in life where waiting was no longer a trial. It was a respite. He wanted to tilt the banana-shaped dish to drink the gooey liquid, chocolate syrup, caramel, butterscotch, and melted whipped cream. He didn't have a spoon—the waitress took it—so he did, he drank it. He figured the waiting thing wasn't necessarily wisdom. He was just tired, and the gooey syrup was good.

Ralphie saw Naum tilt the dish and said, "I'm doing that too."

Naum dabbed with a napkin when she pointed to his beard.

"Next," Coleen said, "I ask to be real. Here I am, such a nice girl in front of my icon corner at home, trying to get the *psyche* and the *soma* into some kind of harmony after cleaning the house, grocery shopping, taking Raphael to school and the dentist and all his other appointments—thank God we have those blessings. God have mercy on people who don't have all that. I'm not complaining.

"And then there's trying to support my husband. The people will say things to the matushka they'd never say to the priest. I took dressmaking in school. He's so particular about his vestments. I try to earn a little extra making cassocks and vestments for the other clergy. Truth be told, if it wasn't for my job at the supermarket, we wouldn't even have health benefits. What would I have done here tonight?

"Then I like to call my mom every day, and my sisters once in a while. And a consistent prayer life, time alone with God? I wonder, can a person be alone with God? Is that possible? Well, anyhow, here's nice little Coleen praying, and half an hour later I'm yelling at some old guy driving too slow who cut me off on the highway when I'm in a hurry to pick up James."

Naum pointed to himself and said, "I'm that old guy."

Coleen had a contagious smile. "No offense. Sorry. But you know what I mean. I don't want to be a phony in front of God. I always ask, Let me be real, please, Lord. Like He doesn't know anyway. 'Oh, what a nice person that Coleen is.' And ten seconds later He's saying, 'No. That woman with the road rage yelling at the old guy in the car can't be the same woman.' So I just pray, Lord, let me be honest about who and where I am in my life in Christ."

"Not easy," Naum said. "So I have a question. We can talk about it another time, but I know a man who was one way when he was young. Another in his middle years. And different again in old age. One way with his wife. Another at work. With his kids. At church. Infant. Prime of life. Decrepit old age. Which one is the real man?"

Coleen said she'd pray about that one, but for now, "How about all of 'em?"

Ralphie had his head on the Formica tabletop. Coleen was pretty sure he was sleeping. Naum noticed and said, "Time to get back to the hotel."

"Last thing?" she said. "Shall I tell you?"

"I was hoping you could. But Ralphie comes first," Naum said.

"Short," she said. "The last thing is asking for stillness. Too many times we get up after praying and say, 'He never answers. It's like I'm talking to myself in the dark, yakking at the ceiling.' But that's because the noise of our everyday life just takes over. It even invades our prayer. So the last thing I ask for is stillness. Then maybe I have a chance to hear the still, small voice."

And, behold . . . after the fire, a still, small voice. And it was so, when Elijah heard it, that he wrapped his face in his mantle.

Naum knew that if after thirty years of prayer God granted three seconds of *hesychia*, of stillness, that was a lot.

Be still, and know that I am God.

"Easier said than done," Naum said.

"Never do it on your own," the young matushka said. "Gotta ask and ask, pray and pray, again and again, like in the Liturgy, like the persistent widow."

Naum looked at Ralphie. "Three stitches," he said.

Coleen said, "All it takes. Three-stitch prayer." And she held up a finger for each. "Pray for prayer. Pray to be real. Pray for stillness so you can hear His voice."

Whether Naum had Zipporah, the wife of Moses, in mind when he visited the seminary and advised the seminarians not to marry a *religious* girl, we never knew, but he did tell 'em, "Ya wanna see a good matushka?" And then he'd nod toward Ralphie's mom singing in the choir over on the kliros and say, "Father James got lucky."

That night, in the ice cream shop, he said to Coleen, "Ya want me to carry him?" Naum looked at Ralphie asleep over the sticky Formica tabletop.

Coleen stood and lifted her sleeping son into her arms. "I got it." She smiled at Naum and said, "And give me that bloody banquet napkin hanging out of your pocket, will ya, Naum? I'm gonna make *Father* a new skufia."

Salvaged

———•———

A RETIRED COP WHO DRANK TOO MUCH, that's how he
became Harry the Hobo or Billy the Bum, depending which
day ya asked him, with the long hair and the big white beard,
sitting wide-eyed outside the cyclone fence on the other side of
the tracks too early in the day to be loaded, and here comes those
goddamn junkyard dogs, three of 'em, a black guy in the lead,
being chased through the auto body scrap heaps.

A short fella and two tall white guys in greasy overalls on his
tail. Black dude does a running leap at the fence and lands halfway up, fingers and boot toes in the crosshatch, dogs bouncing on
their back legs like springboks. The whites all yelling bloody hell.
Then the guy flat-top rolls it over the razor wire at the top of the
fence, and the two tall ones give up trying and just hang desper-
ate there on the cyclone.

But not the short white one. Uh-uh. He slides under a slip
probably dug by the dogs at the bottom. Hell of a thing happened
next . . .

———•———

HARRY. LITTLE HARRY, not the father, Big Harry, but Little Harry, the son, came to see Naum. "Father," he said. "Can I talk with ya?" Wearing his backward Cotton Ball cap, wiping his work boots on the mat, smearing junkyard grease on his dirty blue Red Kap overalls before kissing the priest's hand.

Little Harry knew car parts. All his years in the junkyard? Be a shame if he didn't. That lot? That dirty, greased-down, hard-pack lot? Not even weeds'd grow there. Birds only sat up and looked down from the wires. Rats avoided it. A square city block, maybe more.

Piles and piles and rows and rows of rusted-out junkers and busted-down jalopies. Stacks and mounds of heaped-up axles, bumpers, deck lids, and doors. Every salvaged souvenir of a wreck worth salvaging.

Harry knew 'em all. He worked the counter. Roamed the aisles. Topped the razor wire and fed the dogs. He inventoried parts and logged them in the computer when the operation went U-Pull-It and lit up online.

Harry moved whatever needed moving around the wrecking yard, operated the long-fork forklift like he was born swinging in its longitudinal stability cradle. The little man swung the electro-magnetic crane, cubed hulks in the hydraulic bailer good as any-body, was on a first-name basis with every salvage fork, dumpster bucket, and grapple. The little man knew just how to massage the four-car crusher so she'd let him slip five.

Harry had a friend at the yard they called Getzy.

"Father Naum," Harry said, "Getzy got some bad news. He drinks too much. Smokes a little smoke on breaks. Tends to get excitable, ya know, the stuff they're smoking nowadays, laced with the same stuff they use over at Donahue's Funeral to juice the stiffs? Started using when he was over there in Mogadishu in '92 with the Marines. They tell Getzy, hell no, no custody, joint or otherwise, and no visitation either with his daughter, Claudia, from his first marriage."

Harry told the priest, "Getzy climbs the fence out of the yard, right over the razor-wire past the dogs. Here comes the train, I'm running toward him, me and two other guys, he lays his head on the tracks. I'm the only one not climbing the cyclone trying to get over to him. I got a slit where I go under.

"By the time I get to him, he's still blinking. Half the back o' his head is gone. Says, 'I didn't mean ta do it, Har.' The other guys, fingers in the fence, hanging halfway between, can't believe what they're seeing. Now, nobody'll bury a suicide, Father. The priest where the family grew up says so. And Getzy, Father, you know him, he's been here, coupla times, 'member, last Lent? You know he's not Orthodox."

Naum said, "Harry, was it a suicide?"

Harry said, "If it was, it was unintentional, and slow."

————·————

LITTLE HARRY NEVER MISSED A SUNDAY at Saint Alexander's from when he was a kid. Still served in the altar. Still fit the same server's robe he wore when he was twelve. He just never grew, except out. Betty, his mom—she was Catholic, she told him it wouldn't hurt to drink five cans a night instead of the whole six-pack—she let his robe out around the middle.

Nothing more Harry could do about his serving robe than about the grease under his fingernails. That robe was the one he liked to wear from when he was a kid, the one he'd grown up in and into. A permanent condition, sometimes ya just gotta accept—like the sleeves being up by his elbows and the hem just below his knees. Looked odd when he wore shorts in the summer. But he loved that robe.

Naum never said a thing about it to Harry, except what he said to everybody who came. "Happy just to see you, Haralambos."

A good part of Harry's hair was gone, but he didn't seem to mind. He was always smiling anyway, most of the time.

Getzy—turns out his name was Geert Getzinger—was Harry's best friend. Met in kindergarten. Walked to school together. Had a crush on the same girl in eighth grade, Alita Jean Logwinock.

Harry was Getzy's best man, at both his weddings. Getzy never understood why Harry didn't marry Alita Logwinock, the one love of his life. Harry never told Getzy. By the time Alita got back from the Navy in her hospital corpsman summer whites, men were off the menu. Told Harry, "Call me Doc." Broke Harry's heart.

Sometimes in the junkyard Getzy'd tease Little Harry about Alita. Tease him about going to church all the time too. "Alita dumping ya make ya some kinda monk?"

Hurt like hell. But Harry'd never say so.

Same that day on the tracks, with everybody else on the other side of the fence, nobody wanting to go over, train rumbling away—engineer never even knew. Everybody yelling through the wire, "What's he saying, Har?"

Harry on his knees, holding his friend's head in his lap, trying to keep Getzy together, taking handfuls of blood, praying real quiet, and dripping it three times over Getzy. Harry never said a word to anybody. Told Naum later, "Can a person like me hear some other guy's last confession, or baptize a guy if he asks?"

Naum remembered Geert Getzinger. Harry'd brought him to church, Lent and Pascha two years in a row, and a few other times too. Harry told Naum, "I'm like a link to the wrecks in the junkyard, like an oxygen sensor connector in an engine, except it's to the church, sort of."

Getzy stood there in the side room off the altar. Said he wasn't clean enough to come in. Said he smelled like greasy dirt. Permanent greasy dirt. "Not that you could see the grime on me anyway. Don't matter how hard I scrub." Getzy wasn't the only black man at the yard, but he was probably the most dark-skinned.

The man just stood in that side room, stood the whole time, the whole Liturgy, never took his eyes off what Naum was doing, seeing what could not be seen. Just stood and watched.

Naum saw Getzy. Man had tears in his eyes. Every time Harry made the cross, Getzy did too.

———•———

MICHAEL, OUR CHANTER, when he saw the crowd that morning, told Lefty at the candle stand, "I don't know if there's another priest coulda handled this thing we got going on in there today."

The pangar was three people deep buying candles. Lefty said, "Dropping big bills and buying a hell of a lot o' candles."

So many candles in the sandbox it was like the narthex had a fireplace.

Outside on the street, there were so many motorcycles and amalgamated spare part crates that Donahue's hearse looked like a silver sun in a solar system of scrapyard stars.

Ronny, guy with the ponytail? Him and the one they call Smiley, 'cause nobody'd never seen him smile? They come out on the pavement to have a cigarette.

Smiley's got the whole white shirt, black suit and tie thing going on, hair combed and everything. He says to Ronny, "Looks good, don't he?"

"No. He looks dead," Ronny says.

Smiley just blinks, says, "I mean for a guy who did what he did."

Ronny flicks the cigarette and says, "C'mon, back inside."

"Well, he don't look like one o' these Orthodox." Smiley squirms out of Ronny's grip on his upper arm.

Ronny thumps him on the head. "Yeah, like you'd know."

Many times, Naum had known a church full of Orthodox mourners not to stand, make the cross, or quiet down when the bell rang and the priest parted the curtain of the Royal Doors at the start of a funeral. Seen it many times and wondered why. Grief, maybe, made people forget?

Harry started the bell. Naum parted the curtains. What had been a hushed assembly suddenly rose, all at the same time, and the shared stillness stood with them like an honor guard at attention.

Long-haired bearded riders. Old women with dangling earrings, tight gray braids, and long skirts. Black folks in traditional Sunday garb. Ladies in hats. Black folks in casual dress. White folks in dungarees, sneakers, and tees. Men of all kinds in suits of all colors, some with ties. Young women in short dresses, heels, and patent leather pocketbooks. Children with their heads together, every ethnic kid on the block. Naum swore they were icons of defiance, three steps from the Garden, these children, whispering and snickering, refusing to be shepherded by death.

Workmen from the yard. Tattoos. Piercings. Biker patches, gang-colored do-rags, and caps. Denim. Silk. Cotton. Wool and hemp. Work boots and cleats. Sandaled bare feet. Shoes shiny and spit-polished finer than a newly minted dime.

A group of dress-blue Marines with flags stood for Getzy's honor guard. Veterans in uniform, men and women, young and otherwise. One hospital corpsman.

The owner of the junkyard, Mike Moosher, stood in the back at parade rest—the guy they called Masher, work cap in hand. The family who owned Hop Shing, our local Chinese, across from the yard. Naum recognized a police officer or two by the door. The neighborhood doctor who still made house calls, Doctor Baks, and a lone man weeping, handkerchief in hand. Later it turned out he had been at the controls of the train.

Naum went to the widow, a blonde woman, standing with two light-skinned, gray-eyed children, a boy and a girl, neither one more than seven. They were in the front pew on the side of the church in front of the icon of Christ.

"I'm so sorry, Naomi." She looked shaky. Naum said, "Why don't you sit?"

She said, "No, Father. Thank you." The kids in their Sunday clothes sat bunched close together, pointing through the swirls of incense, sizing up the icons, swinging their legs.

Naum knew the little girl with Naomi was not Claudia, the one from the custody hearing. He knew that child may have been there too, but he didn't ask.

He stood before the people. He thanked them for coming.

They stood, looking at the man whose attire was just as strange to them as theirs was to him. The black under-cassock, the wide-sleeved riason, the purple stole down front almost touching the floor, the phelonion like a cape over his body, the black skufia, his beard, long and white as any man's there.

Facing them, Naum raised his hands and intoned the *Kyrie Eleison* in Greek. He chanted it thirty-three times. Then he said to the people, "Pray it with me for our friend, Getzy."

At first, the crowd was transfixed by the atonal chant. But now, like a great crested wave that one can see rising far off in the sea and coming slowly to shore, all the people joined in as if they had always carried this prayer somewhere inside and were now just so happy to be in a place where it finally made sense to give it voice at last, raising the *Kyrie* along with Naum. He closed his eyes, thinking, *If only.*

Over their prayer, he called, "Please, brothers and sisters,"—he could hardly say it for tears—"don't stop."

Naum, censer in hand, began the petitions over the prayer of the people, who seemed to him so much to want to hope.

———•———

HARRY STOOD SINGING with Naomi and the kids. The icon of Saint Moses the Ethiopian was in the coffin by Getzy. Harry had given it to Getzy back when Getzy told his friend he wanted to be Orthodox, Pascha night, when Deacon Dionysios had Getzy lead the procession carrying the cross.

Back then Naum said to Harry, "Not easy being an icon where you work, eh, Har?"

Harry said to Naum, "Ya think?"

Mrs. Getzinger, Getzy's mom, was there, standing in the front pew on the side of the church in front of the icon of the Theotokos. Three daughters were with her. They were tall, all three women. All in black. They surrounded Naum when he went to them. He almost broke in their embrace.

Naum learned later that Getzy's father had been a German soldier who fell in love with a young woman from our town. He was one of more than four hundred thousand POWs held in almost seven hundred camps in America.

Back home after the war, he couldn't stop thinking about the dark-skinned American girl with the gap between her upper front teeth who worked at the camp where he had been held. He had to find her. It was years ago now since they lost Geert Senior, husband and father, in an accident at the scrapyard.

After, Naum did not accompany the family to the graveyard. The prayers at the church lasted only twenty minutes. He was not able to pray the prayer of absolution. God knows the truth.

Before they left, he spoke with the people. He asked them, "Please, sit."

But they would not.

"Okay, then." Naum said, "I promise not to be long. Just a few words."

He told them about the Shepherd of Hermes, from the late first or mid-second century, considered canonical scripture by early Christians. It came after the Acts of the Apostles in the first New Testament.

Naum read to the people.

These have sinned, and desire to repent, therefore they were not cast to a great distance from the tower, because they will be useful for the building, if they repent.

They then that shall repent, if they repent, will be strong in the faith, if they repent now while the tower is building. But if the building shall be finished . . .

When Naum looked up, a curly-haired, gangly girl who hadn't been there before, a girl in a white dress with Getzy's eyes, stood between the three sisters, never taking her eyes off what was happening, seeing what could not be seen from the pew where Getzy's mother stood. Claudia. Naum knew that child must have been there, but he didn't ask.

He took a moment. Then he said, "Just having people who loved him"—Naum looked at Getzy's wife, his mother, his sisters, Claudia, and the children—"and friends like all of you, and having a friend who had hope"—Naum looked at Harry—"a friend who loved him, just knowing that, gave Getzy hope.

"Here was a man, Getzy, our Getzy, who knew how to salvage parts from wrecks. How to put those parts to good use. A man who knew God didn't make nobody to be a throwaway. A Marine who stood with other Marines and was wounded . . . That's why, in the end, this wounded man—and who do any of us know who isn't walking around wounded?—that's why Getzy hoped, came here, to this church, and shouted with us in the face of our common woundedness, 'Christ is risen, truly He is risen!' The man made that simple confession of faith, here, two Lents and Paschas in a row, and down deep, in spite of everything, he knew the truth, and with his final breath reached out in hope to the Resurrection of our Lord Jesus Christ."

Naum called Dennis Donahue and the funeral staff forward. Dennis instructed the people how things were to proceed.

Then Naum asked Michael the chanter and the little choir to pray the resurrectional hymn as the people came forward to pay their respects to the family and to Getzy, Geert Getzinger, named after his father.

In the flesh Thou didst fall asleep as a mortal man, O King and God. On the third day Thou didst rise again, raising Adam from corruption and destroying death, O Pascha of incorruption, the salvation of the world.

To a person, the people told Harry at the memorial meal—they all said it pretty much the same. But Ronny, the former Secret Service guy? The one who flew rescue choppers in Vietnam? Tall dude, smokes cigars, with the gray ponytail, little Van Dyke beard with the earring, who wore Hawaiian shirts and sandals even in the winter, even for the funeral—he said it best, standing there next to Smiley. He said, "Well, Harry, when heaven eventually does touch down to salvage this scrapheap, at least now the wounded'll know which tower where it's gonna land."

Stole Money

—————•————

IT USED TO BE THAT HE CAME HOME with a *suitcase* full of money, what we heard. Not anymore. Not since moving to our parish. Every year at the Great Blessing of Water at Theophany, he'd go house to house, asking God's blessing on every home and family in the church community.

"It helped," his wife, Greta, said.

He knew the stole money helped. On his salary they barely made ends meet. The ones and fives people gave allowed the family to have little extras. New shoes. A coupla jelly doughnuts here and there. A tree at Nativity and a couple of gifts for the kids. New school clothes. Not that the hand-me-downs from the parish weren't appreciated. Something for Greta on their anniversary. A Friday night date at the local pizza joint. Most of the time they brought the kids. Trusted sitters weren't so easy to find. Maybe a Walmart throw rug to keep off the chill in the bedrooms. One less late notice or utilities shut-off warning. A new-used tire with a little more tread than the bald ones riding on the bent rims of his old beater. I mean, Naum did use that old car to visit all of us. And never mind a vacation. Not unless Matushka

Greta's mom invited them and offered to pay the freight.

Stole money.

The epitrahilion, that's what he called it—the long cloth stole with all the little threaded fringes he said represented God's people. That's what he always called us, God's people, the people he was ordained to serve.

Fancy-looking thing, embroidered down the front. Different color different times of year. Seven crosses on it, hanging down from the neck of his collar to the hem of his cassock, almost to the floor. Practically down to his feet. Surprised Naum didn't trip on it, clumsy as he was, lumbering in his work boots. Steel-toed things are heavy if ya ain't used to 'em when ya first put 'em on. Look funny too, those boots, with his priest get-up. Of all his priest stuff, I think Naum loved that stole most of all. Got it from an old priftereshe whose priest husband died. He made the cross over it, kissed it, said,

Blessed is God, who pours out His grace upon His priests, as myrrh upon the head, which runs down upon the beard, the beard of Aaron, down to the fringe of his raiment,

and put it around his neck before making the prayers.

Same piece of equipment he draped over your head, covered you, when you and him bowed together to pray for forgiveness in front of the cross and the Book of the Gospels. The stole. The sign of God's priesthood. Like Aaron's ephod, Naum always wore it when he prayed for God's people.

Sometimes our people made an offering. They gave the priest money. Stole money. It made some of us feel one way, some another.

"Two things you can always count on," old Vasil Vasili used to say. "Death, and the priest having his hand out."

"Well," Al Anton said, "he's the middleman between us and God. Gotta get his cut."

But few of us understood there wasn't enough money in the neighborhood Police and Fireman's Benevolent Credit Union to pay for what God gave us. And some of us who'd been in the military knew the thing about soldiers not serving at their own expense.

We knew the priest and his family couldn't live on leftover bread, "instead of the gift." That's what we called the portion of the holy bread that wasn't used for Holy Communion—nafora, antidoron.

And we knew we had to free up Father's time so he could be prepared and available to take care of us. I mean, geez, there was lots of us and only one o' him.

I guess it was the way a lot of us saw the transactional nature of what old Vasil Vasili called *the deal* that made Naum feel the stamp of SIMONY hot across his forehead. And even though most of us didn't know what Naum meant by simony, we had no doubt this particular priest wasn't in it for the money.

When Al Anton asked him, "So then why'd ya become a priest? You didn't know this going in?" Naum said someone said it was the uniforms that made him do it, become a priest.

Vasil Vasili knew a lot of priests. His grandfather was a priest back in the old country, an oikonomos, an elevated archpriest. When Naum was ordained, it was Vasil Vasili tugged his collar and told him, "My grandfather the oikonomos knew a thing about managing a franchise, kid. Milk it for all ya can get."

Bothered Naum.

Told Greta his wife, "Maybe I need to reexamine my motives vis-a-vis money and talk with my confessor. Maybe I'm harboring some kind of mercenary guilt. Maybe deep down I do covet money. Maybe it's not the practice of stole money. Maybe it's me."

He wrestled every day with the questions of *sloth, lust of power, and idle talk,* not pulling his hand away when the pious nunnas kissed it.

But the money thing? He knew that needed working on.

Having coffee after the Clergy Brotherhood meeting, Naum was overheard telling another priest he'd decided to no longer accept stole money.

"You do that and you'll make the rest of us look bad," was pretty much the consensus at the meeting.

One of the older priests told him, "We need it. We're already serving like Lazarus at the gate. If it wasn't for Matushka working we wouldn't even have health coverage or be able to keep the heat on in the house. The woman subsidizes the parish's ability to have a priest for God's sake, and I'm not taking His name in vain there either. Half the time I'm lying in bed wondering if old so-and-so in the parish is gonna die, God forgive me, 'cause then with the funeral honorarium I can afford to pay my life insurance in case I die. At least my wife'll have *something.*"

Naum couldn't help it. Something about the current practice and the way it played out in our parish bothered him. He couldn't put his finger on *what,* but something about it wasn't building up our people in the faith. Something about it was making the whole thing sour. There had to be some kind of middle ground, some antidote to feeling spiritually harassed by the worldly quid pro quo.

He decided to do it quietly and explain to the people that while the Fathers said it was prideful not to accept what was offered, he had nonetheless spoken to his confessor, and, for a time at least, until the people could get better and grow together in the Christian practice of giving, no more stole money.

He told the people, "If you want to give money, give it to the church, or to the poor, or to your favorite charity, or maybe somebody in the neighborhood you know's in need."

Somebody had to restore the dynamic.

Secretly, incognito, what he figured he'd do, Naum, he'd get a job maybe where nobody knew he was a priest. Somebody said Greta cried when she saw him in a shirt and tie for the first time in years.

He tried to make her laugh.

"I'm that ugly?" he said.

"Yes, but it's the tie that's really ugly. And old."

Truth be told, he missed wearing a tie. He figured this was as good an excuse as any, going job hunting.

A degree in theology and two-fifty'll get ya a ride on the 47 trolley, maybe. So the guy with the beard in the shirt and tie wasn't surprised, not surprised at all, at the number of polite smiles and pleasant rejections.

First day at seminary they'd told them, you're gonna have to get to be experts in rejection. *If they rejected your Lord* . . .

But it was going with the voucher from the putty factory for the steel-toed work boots after they surprised him and hired him . . . "Cost o' the boots'll come out of your first paycheck," they said. Not that . . .

It was trying on those boots, that right there, that was the surprise. Feeling their weight, lacing up the reality of actually being vested in the fabric of the factory, no iconostasis between him and a crew of men who knew about his other life but had no inclination to kiss his hand, having to suit up and show up, do what he was told and punch the clock, ask permission *first* from the foreman to use the facilities, eat a bagged lunch on the loading dock with putty under his nails and solvent in his nostrils, grind it out till quitting time, go home dirty and dog-tired, the prayer with every breath and heartbeat to survive the day-to-day, gray-wall reality of his maybe prideful, principled stole-money decision.

Surprised him too that the fringe of the stole reached all the way down to his putty-stained, steel-toed boots . . . *down to the hem of his garment*, all the way to something deep within, to some deep visceral connection between liturgy and life.

Theophany home blessings, his favorite opportunity to be with the people in their homes, to sit and talk, and listen—that kind of stole-money relations, building heart-to-heart stuff would just have to be squeezed in between shifts of being broke in as low man on the putty factory totem pole.

The shifts nobody else wanted—*let the layman with the beard work the overnight*—and the damn mandatory overtime, all that factory time-clock rubric, were squeezed between hospital visits, memorial services, funerals, taking Holy Communion to our people in nursing homes, visits to the graveyard, refereeing marriage spats, finding food and rent money for laid-off families, helping new immigrants navigate America, coaxing teens in off the ledge. All the stole-money pastoral responsibilities that came up in the eucharistic family of Saint Alexander the Whirling

Dervish were squeezed like putty between the cracks.

Low man on the factory totem pole, the layman with the beard for sure'd be down in the pit, breathing in the chemicals, the xylene and turpentine, scraping with steel-bristle brushes and rubbing with solvent-soaked rags, cleaning the three-story funnel, squeezed in between and down the funnel, no doubt.

———•———

WE WERE WAITING when the priest arrived at our house. The dog was in the backyard just like he asked. Apparently Naum didn't like dogs jumping around when he was blessing the house. 'Sides, Boots'd actually nipped him one other visit.

When I got home from work and saw the empty bowl on the kitchen table last January after the first time the priest came, I asked Judy, "Where's the holy water?"

"Where d'ya think?" She looked at the drain.

Well, she didn't know. She'd only been Orthodox a short time back then. I told her, "Least the drains are blessed, I guess."

This year she knew.

I was glad I was gonna be home Saturday morning. They were handing out overtime on the Friday overnight at the factory like Halloween candy, and it's not like we couldn't use the extra cash, so I did a double and got home in time for the priest.

Home blessing and one of Judy's Saturday breakfasts after? Don't get any better.

Judy said the kids were so excited they weren't even watching Saturday morning cartoons. They were watching out the window when Naum's old beater pulled up. Kayla, the little one, said, "Jesus is here."

Why she thought the priest was Jesus? Maybe it was the beard.

ON MY WAY HOME from the overnight I stopped at Schmidt's Bakery for half a dozen jelly doughnuts. Eighty cents apiece for doughnuts that used to be a quarter. I walked in past the Salvation Army guy, a geezer in a reindeer hat ringing a bell on the pavement with his red pot—surprised he's still out there after New Year's—took a number from the thing that gives ya a place in the bakery line, and when she called my number, I said to the woman behind the bakery counter, "Give me half a dozen jellies, powdered sugar."

Well, turned out she ain't got no teeth, and she was having a hell of a time trying to bite off a length o' that string they wrap the boxes in. You'd think she'd be a little happier working around a place that smelled so warm and good. But then again, looked like she was working all alone, and that ain't easy doing the counter, and the prep, and answering phones, and whatever they got her doing in the back. Tall woman. Got the real thin wire glasses and the hairnet thing going on, got that *I'm mad at the world and your number ta get abused is next* ire in her eye, staring at the putty all over me and my steel-toed, factory-issue boots. Skinnier than my Aunt Edna, who Aunt Kitty swore had a tapeworm.

When I asked her for the doughnuts, the curmudgeon behind the counter said to me, "You see any powdered-sugar jelly doughnuts, hon?"

Called me *hon*, but she ain't smiling either when she says it.

I was trying to look past her at the mirror behind the counter, looking around the racks of fruit pies and layer cake and the trays of cookies to see if I could spot any stash there in the back of the counter, 'cause I couldn't see any in the display case, and I figured maybe this was some kind of contest or quiz where ya win an extra doughnut or something if ya can answer her question correctly.

But I didn't, so I said, "No." I took a cookie from the sample of broken-ups on the counter and figured, *Well, now Shirley Temple here's gonna tell me about the secret stash o' jellies she's got in the back.*

Nope. She just stood there giving me the look like I gave her dog fleas, and she said, "Only what's out there. Ya ain't seeing any, ya ain't getting any."

Then I realized I'd interrupted her wrapping those famous Schmidt pound cakes in waxed white paper, 'cause she just turned and went back at it.

I'm talking to her back, and I told her, "Kid, you look like you been doing double duty, here all by yourself. I used to work the overnight here for old man Schmidt when I was a kid. And I just got off doing a double over at Pecora putty. We ain't got it easy, the likes o' me and you."

I don't think I coulda got her ta smile even if she had teeth.

After a minute of standing there twisting the five-dollar bill I found on the pavement outside the factory and examining the label sticking out of her uniform at the nape of her neck, I figured, *Well, okay*, and said, "Thanks, cheery." But I only said the *thanks* part out loud, not the *cheery*.

Outside, I think I made the old Salvation Army guy's day when I stuffed the five in his pot. He rang me all the way back to my car, singing "Rudolph the Red-Nosed Reindeer."

Now this priest? This guy was always smiling. Made ya feel happy when ya saw him. He called everybody "cousin." I had a feeling he thought everybody he met was better than him somehow. Then again, I'm just a civilian. I'm no psycho-theologian. I work on a loading dock. I still can't figure that synergy thing he was talking about, no matter how long Judy keeps me waiting on benches watching the escalator over at the mall.

———•———

JUDY WAS SO PROUD when I got home. I was too. They way she laid the table out? My mother couldn't have found a thing to pick at. Well, maybe she mighta.

You shoulda seen it when the priest set it up. Looked like a little home church. Judy had the best tablecloth we had, the one we used only at Christmas or Thanksgiving. I don't know if it's a doily or crocheted or knitted or lace or some other kind of fancy, creamy-colored, webby-looking thing with fringes, but it's harder to fold than a spider's web. I do know I might've been able to unfold it, but I could never fold it without the threads all getting caught in all the rough little slitted cracks and cuts in my fingers and my hands.

Naum spread a big red cloth over the tablecloth on our dining room table. There was a Bible to one side. An enameled hand cross to the other. Some kind of red prayer book.

I gave him a list of names—the living, and our folks who were with Jesus now. He had a tabletop censer going. The kids were loving that. He let each of them drop a piece of incense on the charcoal.

He asked Judy, "Can the kids light a candle?" Two candles in mini-stands, one on each side at the back end of the table. And in the middle, one of Judy's best bowls. He had her fill it with water. She brought our family icons. A sprig of basil tilted in the bowl. A pretty hefty sprig. More like a bunch or a bouquet, really. The whole thing made the house real quiet. Made it smell like church. It was something to see.

So, he made the cross with his hand over the stole, kissed it, put it around his neck, standing there in his cassock. And the guy started to pray, "Blessed is our God, always, now and ever, and unto ages of ages."

Judy said, "Amen."

I was surprised she did, but the priest wasn't. He read from the Gospel. And then asked me to read the epistle. So I did.

Then he prayed for everybody from the bishop to the president; the police, the fire, and the ambulance squads; people serving in homeless shelters, hospitals, nursing homes, prisons; the teachers in our schools; the young men and women in the armed forces, especially, he said, for those at this hour in harm's way; and then he named half the guys from the office to the loading dock over at the factory.

For all of us in the house, by our names. Then he read the list of names from our list. I could swear they were all standing right there with us.

I wanted to ask him, *Hey! What about the guys at the grocery store and Shooky's Taproom? And the Salvation Army dude in the reindeer hat outside Schmidt's?* But I didn't. And I would've written Shirley Temple's name on the list too if I'da known it, but Judy woulda killed me.

Then he went down a long list of petitions from his book. And after each one, my Judy *and* the kids said, "Lord have mercy." And me, the so-called Orthodox, I did too.

That this water may be sanctified by the power, operation, and descent of the Holy Spirit . . .
Purified by the Holy Trinity . . .
Endowed with the grace of redemption, the blessing of Jordan . . .
Heal all souls and bodies, and banish all evil powers . . .
Through partaking of this water and sprinkling therewith we may become sons and daughters and heirs of the Kingdom of Heaven . . .

Then he dipped the hand cross in the water in the sign of the cross, three times.

O Lord our God, Creator of all things, who has granted unto us the baptismal garment of snowy whiteness by water and the Spirit, send down upon us Thy blessing . . .

Judy said, "Amen."

Then he lined us up—me, Judy, little Kayla, and her big sister, Jordyn—and handed each of us something. Judy, our family icon of the Mother and Child. Jordyn's old enough to carry a candle.

He told her, "Keep it away from your sister's hair."

Kayla wanted to carry an icon like Mommy, so Naum gave her the one of her guardian angel. And me, I got to lead the way with the cross in one hand and the tabletop censer in the other, and off we went parading.

"Every room," he said. "Make a big circuit where you go," he said to me, "and we all will follow and end up back here at the table."

He was singing the whole time, except when he stopped in the kids' bedroom and said, "This must be where Mommy and Daddy sleep."

They're looking at him and at their dolls and toys and all their little-girl stuff and saying, "No!" And laughing.

Bless these children, Lord, Jordyn and Kayla, keep them safe and free from all serious injury, illness, incident, and harm, and out of the hands of those who hate Thee, O God.

Every room, almost, he stopped and said, "Who's that?" And "Wow, that's neat." And we were pointing out and telling about family pictures and trophies and all our stuff that makes us feel at home.

O Lord, save Thy people and bless Thine inheritance, grant victory to the Orthodox over the adversary, and by the virtue of the Cross, preserve Thy habitation.

We were heading back downstairs, rounding the final curve, coming into the home stretch. Everything was ready in the kitchen. Coffee smelled so good. I didn't think he heard me whisper to Judy, "Wish I had a jelly doughnut."

Bless, O Lord, the food and drink of Thy servants and the hands which have prepared it. Bless the fountain of the waters. Fill their stores with every good thing and enough to give to those in

need. Have mercy on those who have not, those who are alone,
the sick and suffering, and remember the poor.

Then outta nowhere Naum said, "And remember, O Lord, Honest John and the folks who work at his grocery store, and Mister Shook and the people at his Taproom. And the good people at Schmidt's."

Judy looked at me like, *Ya happy, wise guy?*

Over each of the doors he made the cross.

Bless those who with faith, reverence, and the fear of God enter
herein. Keep this household in Thy peace.

And back in the dining room he replaced all the items on the table. We stood and kissed the cross. He touched our heads with the basil dipped in the blessed water.

He told us, "Orthodox blessing does not add anything. It reveals what is already true, what is already present. It shows the truth that God has created all things and called them good. Us too."

He took off his stole. He packed his things in his bag. He left us a packet of charcoal and incense. He asked the girls, "Can you please help me to fold and pack up?"

We all had a sip of the blessed water from the bowl. The whole house seemed fresh. You would've thought I'd be tired from pulling a double.

We prayed at breakfast. The girls and Judy went along like it was something we always did. Maybe from then on we'd remember. I couldn't believe it when he pulled the white wax-paper bag outta his satchel and said, "I got the last half-dozen at Schmidt's."

Judy looked at me and told Naum, "Made his day."

I said, "Yeah, I'm a sucker for a jelly doughnut."

Dude left the whole bag too.

The girls waved out the window, me and Judy too.

She had tried to give him money.

He said, "Judy, breakfast was more than enough. Thanks, just for inviting me to come. You gotta know somebody in the neighborhood who could use it." Took off his cassock, got in his old beater, and headed toward the factory ta make his shift.

Somebody who could use it. God forgive me, I was thinking of the lady at Schmidt's with no teeth. Maybe go over there later with the kids. I saw a set of teeth on a windowsill at the factory been sitting there a long time, looked like nobody was using.

Then again, these things gotta be fitted by a dentist, right? I mean, ya can't just pop 'em in. Well, she could use the money for that, couldn't she?

When I told Judy my idea, she said, don't worry about it, she'd handle it.

None of us Orthodox on the loading dock ever said a thing when we saw him on the job. We just called him *Urata*, the name we call the priest in our language, so none of the other guys'd give him, or us, any more grief than they already did.

And nobody at the house, not even Kayla, said anything about the putty on his steel-toed work boots, or the xylene or turpentine solvent, or whatever smell was all in his beard and his clothes.

F ATHER STEPHEN N. SINIARI is a priest of the OCA Dio-
cese of the South. During almost forty years in ministry, Fr.
Stephen served parishes in New England and the Philadelphia/
South Jersey area while working full time for an international
agency as a street outreach worker, serving homeless, at-risk, and
trafficked teens. Born and raised in Philadelphia, Fr. Stephen
currently lives on the Florida Gulf Coast with Margot, his wife
of more than forty years.

Ancient Faith Publishing hopes you have enjoyed and bene-
fited from this book. The proceeds from the sales of our books
only partially cover the costs of operating our nonprofit ministry—which includes both the work of **Ancient Faith Publishing** and the work of **Ancient Faith Radio**. Your financial support makes it possible to continue this ministry both in print
and online. Donations are tax-deductible and can be made at
www.ancientfaith.com.

To view our other publications,
please visit our website: **store.ancientfaith.com**

Bringing you Orthodox Christian music, readings,
prayers, teaching, and podcasts 24 hours a day since 2004 at
www.ancientfaith.com